## 'Maia?'

The rounded vowels of his English accent were instantly recognisable. No one else made her name sound like he did—sexy and desirable, full of promise and suggestion.

'Maia?'

His voice repeated her name and this time she turned around. Three years evaporated in the blink of an eye as her past collided with her present.

Henry was standing in front of her.

He looked exactly the same. Tall, dark, and still the most beautiful man she'd ever seen. His features were faultlessly symmetrical. His square jaw was chiselled and his full lips were perfectly shaped. He looked just as she remembered. His hair was cut shorter than usual, his dark curls tamed, but he was otherwise unchanged. He was incredibly gorgeous and he was standing five feet away, when she'd thought he was on the other side of the world.

She wanted to reach out and touch him, to see if he really was real, to make sure it wasn't her imagination playing tricks on her. If it was, it was extremely good. She resisted the temptation.

'I'm back.'

Maia's heart skipped a beat.

Dear Reader,

I have visited Christchurch on New Zealand's South Island several times. It is a beautiful city, but one which experiences a phenomenal number of earthquakes each year, and between September 2010 and June 2011 the city was left devastated by three powerful quakes. I was there in October 2010, not long after the first quake, and saw for myself the damage that Mother Nature can wreak. But along with the heartache and tragedy there were amazing stories of courage, survival and resilience, and Christchurch and her people are slowly recovering.

This is Maia's story, and it was inspired after talking to survivors of the quake: those who had chosen to stay and rebuild their city despite the dangers.

Maia thinks she's happy with her life—until it's turned upside down by two major upheavals. One is the return of her ex—a man who could once make her knees go weak with just a glance, and it seems as if nothing has changed in that respect. And the second is a devastating earthquake. These events force Maia to examine what she really wants out of life, but making a decision is difficult when she knows people are going to get hurt. Her head and her heart aren't always in agreement, and she's struggling to decide which one she should listen to. What if there's more than one right answer?

But Maia has to make a decision—because if she waits too long she could lose everything.

Enjoy!

*Emily*

# A LOVE
# AGAINST ALL ODDS

### BY
### EMILY FORBES

MILLS
BOON

First published in Great Britain 2016
By Mills & Boon, an imprint of HarperCollins*Publishers*
1 London Bridge Street, London, SE1 9GF

Large Print edition 2016

© 2016 Emily Forbes

ISBN: 978-0-263-26105-9

Printed and bound in Great Britain
by CPI Antony Rowe, Chippenham, Wiltshire

**Emily Forbes** is an award-winning author of Medical Romances for Mills & Boon. She has written over 25 books, and has twice been a finalist in the Australian Romantic Book of the Year Award, which she won in 2013 for her novel *Sydney Harbour Hospital: Bella's Wishlist*. You can get in touch with Emily at emilyforbes@internode.on.net or visit her website at emily-forbesauthor.com.

## Books by Emily Forbes
## Mills & Boon Medical Romance

### *Tempted & Tamed!*

*A Doctor by Day…*
*Tamed by the Renegade*


*The Playboy Firefighter's Proposal*
*Wanted: A Father for her Twins*
*Dr Drop-Dead Gorgeous*
*Navy Officer to Family Man*
*Breaking Her No-Dates Rule*
*Georgie's Big Greek Wedding?*
*Sydney Harbour Hospital: Bella's Wishlist*
*Breaking the Playboy's Rules*
*Daring to Date Dr Celebrity*
*The Honourable Army Doc*
*A Kiss to Melt Her Heart*
*His Little Christmas Miracle*

Visit the Author Profile page at millsandboon.co.uk for more titles.

For my gorgeous nieces:
Sophie, Lucy, Kate, Sophie, Grace, Zoe,
Harriet, Portia, Lilly, Saskia, Henriette,
Alexandra, Charlotte, Georgia and Adelaide,
and in loving memory of Georgiana Rose.

**Praise for
Emily Forbes**

'…a very interesting medical romance
because of a unique setting and really
different medical situations.'

—*HarlequinJunkie* on
*A Kiss to Melt Her Heart*

# CHAPTER ONE

'CHRISTCHURCH HAS BEEN *rocked by the biggest earthquake we've had for some time. Just after five o'clock this morning a quake measuring seven-point-one on the Richter scale was recorded; its epicentre was forty kilometres west of the city and it occurred at a depth of eleven kilometres. Several old buildings have collapsed but, while there have been numerous injuries, there are no reported fatalities at this stage. Injuries have been caused by falling masonry and glass but—just repeating—there are no fatalities at present. We're crossing live now to our reporter...'*

Maia Tahana pulled the headphones out of her ears as she walked through the automatic doors of the emergency department of the Canterbury

Children's Hospital, cutting the radio journalist off midsentence. The story of the quake wasn't news to her; she'd been woken by it, jolted out of a comfortable sleep by a deep bass rumble and the sound of breaking glass. Her heart had hammered in her chest as the house shook and the windows rattled in their frames. It had sounded as if a freight train was hurtling past the front door but Maia had known that was impossible. The closest thing to the house was the Pacific Ocean, fifty metres away on the other side of the sand dunes that ran at the bottom of the garden—but it hadn't been the pounding of the surf that had shaken the house and its foundations.

The noise had been frightening and the movement of the house disturbing but it wasn't an unfamiliar experience. Maia had lived in Christchurch, New Zealand, all her life; she'd been through this before. Christchurch experienced thousands of earthquakes each year. She remembered hearing it was somewhere in the vicinity of thirteen thousand, which seemed like an enormous number, but she knew that not all of them were felt by people. Some were only detected by seismic equipment, but it was still a huge number, and it wasn't unusual around here to feel the ground moving beneath your feet.

Minor quakes were something that barely caused the locals to blink, let alone miss a beat. If the power wasn't interrupted, if no one was hurt and if there was no major damage, then the tremors were mostly ignored. But this one had been big and much closer to the surface. There had been a couple of smaller aftershocks and Maia was pleased to hear there had been no fatalities. Perhaps she could expect a regular shift, if ever there was such a thing for an emergency-department nurse in a busy paediatric hospital.

The emergency department seemed quiet when Maia walked in but she was superstitious enough not to say anything. The moment someone mentioned the 'q' word always seemed to be the moment all hell broke loose. She decided to grab a coffee while she had a chance. She needed a double dose of caffeine after being woken by the quake. She and her sisters had been sweeping up broken crockery and glass since four this morning and she hadn't had a chance to go back to sleep. She checked her watch. She had time.

She walked into the empty kitchen and took a coffee cup from the cupboard. She had her back to the kitchen door but she heard it open as she lifted a new pod from the box on the bench beside the coffee machine. The room filled with the scent of cedar wood and citrus—grapefruit, not oranges. The scent was familiar to her. It was the scent of an ex-boyfriend. She closed her eyes and breathed deeply, letting the memories flood back. A slight smile played across her lips as she remembered Henry.

She opened her eyes and mentally shook herself. She didn't have time to waste on old memories. She dropped the coffee pod into the machine, waiting for the aroma of freshly brewed coffee to clear her mind. Henry was a long time ago. He was her past. Well and truly. Her life had moved on. She had changed. Life had changed her.

But as she pushed the button to start the coffee-making process she could have sworn she heard his voice.

'Maia?'

The rounded vowels of his English accent were instantly recognisable. No one else made her name sound like he did—sexy and desirable, full of promise and suggestion.

Her imagination was working overtime.

'Maia?' His voice repeated her name and this time she turned around.

Three years evaporated in the blink of an eye as her past collided with her present.

Henry was standing in front of her.

He looked exactly the same: tall, dark and still the most beautiful man she'd ever seen. His features were faultlessly symmetrical. His square jaw was chiselled and his full lips were perfectly shaped. His indigo-blue eyes were the exact same shade as the chest feathers of the pukeko bird. He stood over six feet and he was solid, but in a lean, muscular way. Not fat. He looked just like she remembered—his hair was cut shorter than usual, his dark curls tamed, but he was otherwise unchanged. He was incredibly gorgeous and he was standing five feet away when she'd thought he was on the other side of the world.

'Henry? What are you doing here?'

She wanted to reach out and touch him, to see if he really was real, to make sure it wasn't her imagination playing tricks on her but, if it was, it was extremely good. She resisted the temptation. She wasn't sure what would be considered appropriate behaviour.

'I'm back.' He smiled at her as he gave her his answer and Maia's heart skipped a beat. He had a little dimple in the centre of his chin that disappeared when he smiled—how had she forgotten about that?

She could see he was back. What she wanted

to know was why and when and how long for but all she could do was stare at him.

'I didn't know you worked here,' he said to her.

Maia nodded. Her mouth was dry and her tongue appeared to have glued itself to the roof of her mouth. She forced it free and swallowed as she tried to moisten her throat so she could speak. 'I left the Queen Liz eighteen months ago,' she told him.

When Henry had left Christchurch three years ago Maia had been working in the emergency department at the Queen Elizabeth Hospital—they both had—but she had quit that job eighteen months ago after her father had passed away. She hadn't wanted to nurse adults anymore; she'd needed a break and the Children's Hospital had needed staff.

'I'm sorry about your dad,' Henry said, putting two and two together with the timing. 'He was a good man.'

Henry had always had an uncanny ability to

read her thoughts and it seemed as if that hadn't changed.

'Thank you,' she said but she didn't want to think about her father. She didn't want to think about the last few months of his life. Her dad had suffered a stroke and Maia had helped to nurse him. It had been a difficult and emotional time, and his death had hit her hard. She had spent a vast amount of the past three years grieving. First for Henry and then for her father. She was only just coming to terms with it all now.

The coffee machine beeped at her and she turned away, grateful for the distraction, grateful for the reason to break eye contact and the chance to gather her thoughts. But her first thought was about Henry.

Why was he back?

The comms system crackled overhead. 'All ED staff to triage.' Maia heard the voice of Brenda, the ED director, summoning the staff.

Her hand shook as she added sugar to her coffee and picked up the cup. Henry held the door open and fell into step beside her. She wasn't going to escape the past that easily.

'What are you doing here?' she asked. When Henry had left Christchurch three years ago she had never expected to see him again. He had never mentioned coming back; he'd made her no promises. He'd gone off to save the world, leaving her behind, and Maia could only assume that she didn't feature in his future plans at all. That had been a bitter pill to swallow but she'd managed to do it eventually.

'I'm doing project work in disaster management and the New Zealand government offered me a grant to come back. I'll be looking at the systems in place in the hospitals and how they would cope with mass-casualty incidents. But I'll be attached to the Children's. I thought it was an offer too good to refuse.'

That surprised her. Not his project choice—he was an emergency-medicine specialist and she'd known about his interest in disaster management—but the fact that he was back at all was a surprise. When he'd left he'd had plans that were bigger than New Zealand.

'Well, your timing couldn't be better,' she told him. 'You got an earthquake to order.'

'Looks like I did but it hasn't caused too much havoc—and, although that's fortunate for Christchurch and her residents, it's not very useful for my purposes.'

'I guess you can't have everything.'

'I guess not.'

Henry's indigo eyes searched her face. He seemed able to look through her brown eyes into her soul and his gaze, intense, powerful and passionate, made her knees go weak. She remembered this look. It was the look he would give her when they'd made love. The look that had made her think she was the only girl in the world he would ever need.

She looked away.

That wasn't the case and she wasn't that girl anymore.

'When did you get back?' she asked.

'A couple of days ago. I spent yesterday in orientation and induction and now I hope I'm ready to go.'

Yesterday she'd been rostered off. Today her world was changing.

As she and Henry assembled in triage along with the other staff, Maia saw Carrie, her best friend, standing on the opposite side of the group. She raised her eyebrows in a silent question at Maia when she saw who was by her side. Maia gave a slight, almost imperceptible shake of her head. She didn't want Carrie asking questions.

'If I can have everyone's attention...' the ED Director said as she scanned the group, obviously deciding everyone was present and accounted for. Brenda waited for the conversational noise to cease before continuing. 'There's been an accident involving a school bus and we've got several ambulances headed our way.'

Maia shouldn't even have *thought* about it being quiet.

'Apparently the earthquake triggered a land-slide which caused the bus to crash but I don't have any more detail than that. The bus driver has been airlifted to the Queen Elizabeth and the plan is to bring all the kids to us. There were sixteen primary school children on the bus. Varying injuries—fractures, cuts, bruises, some suspected head injuries and possible spinal injuries—and all of them will be in shock.' She glanced at the clock on the wall. 'ETA five minutes.'

'It seems you got your disaster after all,' Maia said quietly to Henry as Brenda went on.

'For those of you who haven't met him yet, I'd like to introduce Dr Henry Cavanaugh. Henry is a UK-trained emergency-medicine specialist with a special interest in disaster management. He did part of his fellowship in Christchurch at the Queen Liz but this time he is seconded to our hospital and he will be looking at our management systems, as well as taking on a clinical workload.'

Maia could see Carrie making a beeline for her and by her expression she could tell she was in for a grilling. She really needed to process Henry's return before she was ready for it to be dissected in a discussion with anyone, even her best friend. But she knew her chances of putting Carrie off were next to none so all she could do was ensure that the conversation didn't take place in public.

Henry was about to be swamped by other emergency staff who hadn't yet met him so Maia headed for the change rooms, deciding she would quickly change into surgical scrubs. Carrie followed her, as she'd known she would. She and Carrie had been best friends since their first year of high school. For thirteen years Carrie had been by Maia's side. She'd been through everything that had happened to Maia over the past three years and longer.

The moment the door closed behind them, Carrie asked, 'Did you know he was back?'

Maia stripped off her uniform and hung it on

a spare coat-hanger, exchanging her clothes for hospital-issued scrubs. 'Who? Henry?'

'Yes, Henry,' Carrie replied as Maia stepped into a pair of surgical pants and tied the drawstring at her waist.

'No. You know we haven't kept in touch.' They had agreed on a clean break—that had been his suggestion, not hers—and she'd spoken to him exactly twice in three years. He had called her once when her father had suffered his first stroke and again when he had died. That had been their only contact. Henry wasn't part of her life anymore.

'How did your date go last night?' Maia asked as she tugged the pale-blue cotton shirt down over her head.

'Don't change the subject.'

'I'm not. Henry being back is not a subject. Not one that affects me anyway.'

Carrie raised an eyebrow. 'You sure?'

Even though Maia had known the fairy tale hadn't had the happy ending she'd wanted, and she'd pretended he hadn't broken her heart when he'd left, it had taken her a long time to recover. But eventually she'd been able to consign him to her past and to think of him without feeling like her heart was being ripped in two. They'd wanted different things in life. Things had worked out for the best.

'Positive,' she said as she lifted her hand to gather her long, dark hair into a ponytail, wrapping and tucking the end to make a messy bun. Her engagement ring caught the light, reminding her to remove it, and she slid it off her finger and onto the necklace where she wore it while she was working.

She was engaged to be married. Henry was an ex-boyfriend. Not the love of her life.

'He's an ex-boyfriend, that's all.'

Henry was her past. Not her future.

He wasn't her Henry any more.

# CHAPTER TWO

TWO AMBULANCES PULLED into the loading bay as Maia and Carrie returned to the ED, creating a flurry of activity. Maia's fiancé, Todd, was a paramedic. He had a day shift and she peered through the windows of the closest ambulance and scanned the bustling medicos, looking for his familiar figure. Looking for his sturdy frame, his short, neat brown hair and his gentle hazel eyes.

A girl of about eight or nine was pulled from the back of the first ambulance. There was no sign of Todd. The girl's eyes were closed and she had a firm cervical collar around her neck.

'Carrie, this child needs a neuro consult, possible head injury. Jim Edwards is on his way down but can you monitor her until he arrives?'

Brenda relayed the paramedics' summary of the girl's condition.

'Sure.' Carrie had worked at the Children's since graduating from nursing. She was one of the most experienced emergency nurses and there wasn't much she hadn't had to deal with before. She crossed straight to the first stretcher.

The doors of the second ambulance swung open and Maia saw Todd climb out. She headed for her fiancé, closely followed by Brenda. Despite the fact that he'd just come from what she imagined was a complicated and messy motor-vehicle accident with multiple casualties, Todd looked as immaculate as ever. He was fastidiously neat and somehow his uniform had remained clean and still had perfect creases in the trouser legs. In contrast Maia could sense that her thick dark hair was already escaping from the bun she'd fixed it in. She couldn't count how many times people had uttered the phrase 'opposites attract' when they'd been talking about her and Todd.

He pulled a stretcher from the back of the truck. A young boy was sitting up on it. He was alert and seemed quite fascinated by the whole experience. He was dressed in his school uniform, shorts and a T-shirt, and Maia could see that his left knee was swollen. The paramedics had rolled up a towel and stuffed it under his knee to support it.

'Adam has undiagnosed knee pain,' Todd told them. 'And he's unable to weight bear. Vitals all with normal limits.'

'Henry.' Brenda nodded as she called Henry over to join them. 'Ortho injuries; can you take this one?' she said as she pointed to Adam. 'Maia, you go with him.'

She wondered if that was a coincidence or if Henry had requested to work with her. *Don't flatter yourself*, she remonstrated as Todd handed her a little green whistle-shaped inhaler.

'He's had the Penthrox inhaler on the way here,' he said.

Maia nodded and tucked the pain-reliever

alongside Adam, then put her hands on the stretcher, ready to wheel it away. Before she had moved Todd reached over and gave her shoulder a gentle squeeze. 'I'll see you later,' he said.

Maia saw Henry watching. His eyes moved from Todd's hand to Todd and then to her face. Maia blushed under his scrutiny. She almost felt like she shouldn't have let Todd touch her. Not that she could have stopped him, nor was she sure why she would have wanted to, but his familiar gesture made her feel awkward and uncomfortable under Henry's gaze. His expression was unreadable but he gave the stretcher a push, starting it moving towards the entrance, and Todd's hand dropped from Maia's shoulder with the movement. Henry wasn't watching her now, he was focused on manoeuvring the stretcher, but Maia knew his movement had been deliberate. She said nothing as she and Henry wheeled the stretcher away and Todd turned back to his other patient, to the girl with the broken collarbone.

'Hey there, mate, what's your name?' Henry had always had a good bedside manner and everyone, young and old, loved him. He had an easy charm. People were starstruck by his arresting looks initially but he always won them over with his personality to match.

She needed to be careful. Before he'd left she'd had him on a pedestal; she couldn't let that happen again. But, listening to him chat to their young patient, she could tell he hadn't changed.

'Adam Evans.'

'Nice to meet you, Adam. I'm Henry and this is Maia,' he said. 'You've hurt your knee, have you?'

Adam nodded.

'We'll get you comfortable in here and have a look at it. Have you been in hospital before?'

'No,' he said. Maia grabbed a blank patient file from the triage desk as they wheeled the stretcher past.

'Seen it on telly?'

He nodded again as they pushed his bed into

a cubicle and Maia pulled the curtain around to give them some privacy.

Maia helped Henry transfer Adam to a hospital bed before she wheeled the stretcher into the corridor. She knew one of the ambulance crew would collect it before they left the hospital but she didn't want them to have to interrupt, especially if it was Todd. She wasn't ready to deal with two sets of inquisitive eyes.

'Maia will attach a few leads to you,' Henry told Adam as he washed his hands before pulling on a pair of disposable surgical gloves. 'She'll check your pulse and a few things like that but I reckon that'll all be pretty normal, seeing as you're talking to me.'

They had worked together at the Queen Liz when Henry had been doing his fellowship. They'd worked well together then and slotted back into an easy rhythm now. It didn't feel like three years since they'd worked side by side.

Maia took a hospital ID bracelet out of the file and wrote Adam's details on it before fastening it around his wrist. Next she snapped gloves onto her hands, connected Adam to the monitors and recorded his observations—blood pressure, oxygen sats and pulse rate.

'Do you know what day it is, Adam?' Henry asked as he shone a penlight torch into Adam's eyes and checked his pupils.

'Tuesday.'

'Do you remember what happened?'

'I was standing up in the bus when the driver swerved and I went flying, and my knee slammed into the side of one of the seats. It hit that metal bar that made up the seat frame. My brother was on the bus too. Do you know if he's okay? His name is Bailey.' Tears welled in Adam's eyes and Maia could tell he was trying to be brave. She could imagine how she would have felt if she'd been in his situation at the same age.

'Let's get you sorted and then we'll find out about Bailey,' she told him. She wouldn't tell him that she was sure Bailey was fine; she couldn't promise that when she had no idea of the situation. Promising to investigate was the best she could do.

'All right, Adam, I need to have a look at your knee, but first I want you to tell me about your pain. Can you give it a score out of ten? Where zero is no pain and ten is unbearable.'

'Maybe a six?'

'I need to have a feel of your knee but you can hold Maia's hand if you like and squeeze it tight if your knee gets too sore and you want me to stop. I reckon holding Maia's hand might help.' Adam blushed and looked away and Maia almost felt sorry for him until she realised that Henry had started palpating the knee joint and had successfully distracted Adam so that he'd been able to start palpating without Adam even noticing. Obviously he hadn't struck anything painful yet but as a technique Maia was impressed.

The pain-relieving inhaler was lying where

Maia had left it, on the bed. She picked it up and offered it to him. 'You can use this if you like?'

But Adam shook his head. 'I'll be okay,' he said, still putting on a brave face.

'Good choice, Adam. I'd choose to hold a pretty nurse's hand instead too,' Henry added as he palpated the medial and lateral ligaments and winked at Adam, who grinned. Now it was Maia's turn to blush but she held out her hand and Adam latched onto it.

As the young boy squeezed her hand, Maia wondered if anyone watching her and Henry would guess they had a history. Henry seemed relaxed; working with her didn't appear to be throwing him off-kilter. Perhaps it was only her on tenterhooks, only her who still felt the spark of awareness in the air. There was no denying she was still affected by his easy charm.

Henry moved his fingers centrally over the quadriceps tendon and muscle belly. There was marked oedema of this knee compared to the other and Maia watched as Adam grimaced, but he didn't cry out.

'Are you a cricketer, Adam?' Henry asked.

Adam nodded.

'So, you'd be getting ready to watch the World Cup?'

The World Cup was scheduled to start in India at the end of February. It was only a few days away and New Zealand's citizens could barely talk about anything else. Maia knew that Henry also loved his cricket. He would slot straight back into the Kiwi culture even if he did barrack for the wrong team.

'Do you reckon the Black Caps can beat my team—England?'

Henry was having difficulty finding the borders of the knee cap. Adam flinched and his fingers tightened their grip on Maia's as Henry's fingers probed his patella but his bravado remained strong as he replied, 'The Black Caps can beat everyone.'

'I like your confidence.' Henry laughed. 'I'm

looking forward to watching some cricket. I've been living in America—they're not into cricket there. See if you can bend this knee for me. I'll help you.' Henry had again successfully distracted Adam but his assessment wasn't over yet. He slipped one hand under Adam's knee to support it. It was resting in about thirty degrees of flexion and he was able to bend it another thirty degrees before the pain got too much. But Maia knew that flexion of sixty degrees was well off the normal range of one hundred and forty degrees for thin adolescents.

But Henry praised his efforts. 'Well done, Adam. Now try to straighten it for me.'

Adam tried but he couldn't do it. His knee got stuck at thirty degrees.

'Can you lift it off the bed?'

Maia could see from Adam's expression that he was trying but his quadriceps wasn't following orders and his leg didn't budge.

'These kids are primary school age, yes?'

Henry asked Maia. 'How old are you, Adam?' he asked when she nodded.

'Twelve.'

'All right. I reckon you might have busted your knee cap; we need to get that X-rayed.'

Maia frowned. Patella fractures weren't common in children and she wondered why Henry suspected that. He must have seen her doubting expression. 'I've seen a few in this age group, boys more than girls,' he explained. 'Once the patella has ossified it's susceptible to fracture. Can we organise an X-ray? AP and lateral views?' he asked.

'Sure. They can bring the mobile X-ray machine in to do that. But we'll need to get permission first, I suspect. Why don't you ask Brenda to organise that when you get your next case and I'll wait with Adam?' Maia didn't want to leave the young boy alone. He would be apprehensive, if not scared, and with the added worry of his brother's whereabouts and potential injuries. 'And see what you can find out about

Bailey,' she added as Henry pulled the curtain back and stepped out.

She watched him leave the cubicle. His dark hair was neat at the nape of his neck. His back was straight, his shoulders square. He seemed relaxed, unhurried, in control, and Maia knew his calm demeanour was good for the patients.

Henry turned to pull the curtain closed and saw her watching him. He grinned and winked as he tugged the curtain across, cutting off her view.

Maia busied herself checking Adam's obs again while she waited for the blush that stained her cheeks to fade. She needed something to occupy her mind; she couldn't afford to fill it with thoughts of Henry.

She heard the curtain move again. The sound of the plastic clips sliding in the rail made her look up. She was hoping to see Henry but it was a lady's face that appeared.

'Excuse me,' the woman said as she ducked around the curtain. 'Sorry to interrupt—I'm

Amelia Cooper, the deputy principal at Canterbury Primary School.'

Maia spotted an identification badge hanging around Amelia's neck that had her photograph and the school crest printed on it. She hoped she wasn't a journalist with fake ID. That had happened before, on more than one occasion.

'Hello, Adam,' the woman said, and Maia decided she would give her the benefit of the doubt, although she wasn't sure what she was doing in her cubicle.

'Is there something I can help you with?' Maia asked.

'I need to make sure all the children are accounted for,' Amelia explained. 'The school is contacting the parents. Some are already on their way to the hospital, but I was told we might need permission for some treatments. The school has all that information on file.' She indicated the electronic tablet she held in one hand. 'It's all in here.'

She put the tablet down on the end of Adam's

bed and took a thick marker pen from a clip-board which she had been holding in her other hand. 'I'm also supposed to correctly identify the children,' she said as she printed Adam's name onto a sticky label which she peeled off and stuck to his shirt. Some things obviously still had to be done the old-fashioned way, al-though Maia knew her method of identifying the children was more secure. Adam's arm would go wherever he went, unlike his shirt, which could easily be removed, taking his ID with it. But she kept quiet. The children could be iden-tified at a glance and another form of ID wasn't going to create any problems, as long as it was accurate.

'And I'll keep a list of their injuries so the par-ents can check in with me as their initial point of contact. I'll be the liaison person, according to your ED director that will leave you all free to get on with treating the kids.'

That made sense. Maia filled her in on Adam's condition and Amelia flipped over the page of sticky labels and jotted a summary on another page of her clipboard.

'Do you have authority to give permission for Adam to have an X-ray?' Maia asked.

'I do,' she replied. 'I spoke to Dr Cavanaugh who was in here before and told him.'

'Okay. Do you have any news about Adam's brother, Bailey?'

Amelia ran her finger down the list on her clipboard. 'He's fine. He's got some cuts and bruises and he's waiting for some treatment to clean those up.'

Maia could see Adam relax. 'That's good news, isn't it?'

'I've got more good news, Adam,' Amelia said. 'The school has spoken to your mother and she is on her way.'

The radiographer arrived and Maia left him to do his job while she went looking for Bailey.

The waiting room had filled with parents and some of the less seriously injured kids who were still waiting to be treated. Maia scanned the room and spotted a boy who, despite the large dressing that was bandaged to the top of his head, looked similar enough to Adam that she walked closer to check the sticker on his shirt. It read, 'Bailey Evans'.

Maia sought out the ED Director next. She was standing at the whiteboard behind the triage desk, updating the list. 'Brenda, have you got anyone urgent for me or can I take Bailey Evans?' she asked. 'I've got his brother having X-rays taken and I think they'd like to be together while they wait for their mother.'

Brenda scanned the board quickly before she nodded. 'Sure,' she said as she added a note on the board beside Bailey's name. 'According to the ambos he's got a head laceration that might need stitching. Your call, once you've cleaned him up.'

Maia introduced herself to Bailey as she pushed his wheelchair into the cubicle beside Adam's. They could talk to each other through the curtain while she cleaned Bailey's cuts—she didn't think Adam needed to watch that—but once they were both taken care of she could pull back the curtain and they could wait together.

Maia gently lifted the dressing on Bailey's head. It was soaked in blood from a nasty cut that ran along his hairline. The paramedics had been right; the gash would probably need a few stitches. She re-covered the wound with fresh padding and called for a doctor. The wound would need to be cleaned but she knew the doctor would administer a local anaesthetic and she preferred to wait for that before she started cleaning. She would make a start on his other more straightforward injuries while she waited. She could see several cuts on his hands and knees as well as on his face and head.

'How did you get all of these cuts?' she asked him.

'Some of the windows in the bus exploded when the bus rolled over.'

'The bus rolled over?' Maia hadn't been aware of that part.

Bailey nodded his head.

'The bus driver swerved so hard to miss the landslide that the bus crashed through the rail on the side of the road and rolled down the hill.' Adam's voice came through the curtain, explaining the sequence of events.

'You didn't tell me that part before, Adam.'

'That wasn't the bit where I hurt my knee,' he said matter-of-factly.

'The window next to me smashed,' Bailey added. 'And then some of us had to break the emergency window and crawl out that way. That's how I cut my hands and knees.'

Maia picked fragments of glass out of his wounds, disinfected them and bandaged them before she tackled his face and head. She cleaned the cuts and scratches on his face before she carefully unwrapped the dressing on his head.

The curtain rustled on its tracking, flicking open to admit Henry. 'This is Bailey, Adam's brother,' Maia told him. 'He's got a laceration on his head that needs cleaning and suturing.'

She removed the dressing again for Henry to take a look. He nodded, agreeing with her assessment.

Maia handed him the local anaesthetic, preempting his request, and then prepared a suture kit while they waited for the anaesthetic to kick in. They worked smoothly together, their moves practised as Henry chatted to Bailey about cricket and rugby. Maia loved rugby but didn't really understand the attraction of cricket and she wasn't interested in listening to them discuss their favourite teams and players. She was busy thinking about other things. She was standing beside Henry's right shoulder, snipping the thread each time he finished a stitch. She didn't need to focus; her mind was free to wander and she let it drift as she watched his fingers pinch and move as he deftly sewed up Bailey's head wound.

He looked like he was conducting a mini-orchestra. His hands moved to their own silent beat. His fingers were long and slender, his forearms were strong. He was wearing a short-sleeved surgical top, a dark blue one that made his eyes look even darker than usual, and his olive skin was lightly tanned, even though he'd just returned from a Northern Hemisphere winter. She wondered what colour the skin under his clothes was.

That was a dangerous direction for her thoughts to take. She quickly tried to think about something else. She breathed deeply as she tried to refocus her mind. But all that happened was she breathed in Henry. She was standing so close to him that all she could smell was the scent of clean laundry and that citrus-and-cedar aftershave, and every breath she took filled her senses.

'Henry?'

Brenda stuck her head around the curtain and Maia jumped. She felt a guilty flush steal across her cheeks even though she was guilty of nothing more than wayward thoughts. But Brenda's appearance was enough to break the spell. Maia took a small step back, putting a little bit of distance between Henry and her.

'Adam's X-rays are back.'

'Okay. Can you put the dressing on?' Henry asked as Maia cut the final thread. 'I'll follow up on Adam.'

Henry swapped cubicles and Maia breathed out. She hadn't realised that she'd been holding her breath but it must have been protective tendencies. If she couldn't smell Henry, she could think. It was good that he was gone. She needed a bit of distance. Despite telling herself that Henry's return didn't matter and that it wasn't going to affect her, she knew that was a lie. She hoped he'd spend a lot of time in Theatre and on the wards—anywhere away from Emergency. She didn't know how she could be expected to function normally if she had to work closely with him.

She put a new dressing on Bailey's head and pulled the curtain back so the boys could see each other. Henry had his back to her as he studied Adam's X-rays. He held them up to the light and Maia was about to leave him to it when she heard Carrie's voice on the other side of the curtain, and another stranger came into the cubicle. Another woman. But this time Maia knew immediately who she was. The boys' mother. It wasn't that she looked particularly like them but Maia could tell by the way she rushed in and ignored the adults in the room completely as she sought out her children. Maia might as well have been invisible. The woman hesitated for just a fraction as if trying to choose which of her sons to hug first but chose Bailey. He was closer.

Henry turned around at the sound of a new voice and Maia noted the woman's double-take when she saw Henry. As concerned as she was for her children, part of her, possibly just her female hormones, still couldn't help reacting to Henry. It seemed he wasn't quite as invisible as Maia was. Not that Maia could blame her. There weren't many people, men or women, who were immune to Henry's looks. He was a strikingly handsome man. Maia's glance went instinctively to the woman's left hand to see if she was single. Not that it was any of her business. She tried not to care but she didn't want other people noticing Henry. Although she knew that was impossible.

'Mrs Evans?' Henry queried as the woman kissed Bailey and then moved over to hug Adam. 'I'm Dr Henry Cavanaugh,' he went on when she nodded. 'I'm an emergency specialist at the hospital and Maia and I have been treating your sons. They are both fine. They've sustained relatively minor injuries but, all things considered, they've been very lucky. Bailey has a few small cuts that have been cleaned and dressed but he also had one larger gash on his head which required ten stitches—just here.' Henry touched his own head just at his hairline. 'He'll need to get those out in a week. Your GP might be happy to do it or you can bring him in here.

'Adam has a fractured knee cap,' Henry continued as he slid one of the X-rays into the light box on the wall. This X-ray showed a lateral view and Maia could see the dark line indicating the break running across the middle of Adam's patella. Henry traced his finger over the line. His fingers were slender and capable, his hands smooth and hairless. Maia forced her attention back to the matter at hand and listened as Henry told Mrs Evans what had happened. She needed to pay attention; she would need to write discharge summaries for the boys.

'It's not serious. A transverse fracture of the patella is not particularly common but it matches with Adam's age and the injury history. The physio will be along shortly to fit him with a splint and we'll make an appointment with an orthopod to review his progress in two weeks. He should expect to stay in the splint for four weeks and then he will need physiotherapy. You can take the boys home as soon as the physio has taught him how to use crutches.'

'Adam gets crutches?' Bailey sulked.

The boys' mother laughed. 'Now I know you're okay,' she said.

Henry high-fived both of the boys. 'Maia, can you ring Outpatients and set up a review for Adam in a fortnight?'

Maia nodded. They had worked well together. No awkwardness. There had been no time to worry about anything other than their patients. She was right—Henry being back wasn't going to affect her.

Henry scrubbed his hands as he prepared to go into Theatre, taking a few moments to collect his thoughts. He hadn't had a moment of solitude since he'd bumped into Maia earlier today. If he hadn't been working solidly with her all morning, he could almost have believed he was dreaming. They'd been treating their young patients nonstop for hours, and his day wasn't over yet, but he needed just a little time to think.

He hadn't been completely honest with Maia about his reasons for coming back to Christchurch. He'd been offered a grant, that much was true, but he'd been offered several and he'd accepted Christchurch partly because of her. He hadn't come back *for* her but because of her. He had actually been happy here and he had Maia to thank for that. It had been many years since he'd felt truly happy, before Christchurch or since.

Six years ago his world had collapsed and as he'd recovered he'd made a decision. He would save the world, one disaster at a time, and if he couldn't save the world then he would at least try to make a difference to one family at a time. That had put him on the path to emergency medicine and disaster management. He knew exactly how devastating losing loved ones unexpectedly in traumatic circumstances was and, if he could make a horrible, tragic situation better, then that was what he wanted to do. If it kept him busy day and night, that was a good thing. He had no desire to have a life of his own. His family didn't get that now—why should he?

He'd been rudderless, almost homeless, for six years now. He hadn't wanted to stay in one place; he knew that being settled without any family around would make him feel even more alone. Family couldn't be replaced. Not even by another family. The risk was too great—something might happen to them too.

He'd decided it was better to remain alone, even if it meant being lonely, rather than risk his heart on love.

And then he had met Maia and he'd been tempted to change his mind. But he hadn't been able to ask her to commit to a life of uncertainty with him when he hadn't even been sure if he wanted that commitment. Yet he hadn't been able to resist returning and so he was back in Christchurch. This city held some of his few cheerful memories, without any lurking ghosts, and he was sorely in need of some happiness.

# CHAPTER THREE

MAIA LOOSENED HER hair from the bun she'd worn it in all day and let it fall down her back in thick, dark waves as she and Carrie strolled along the banks of the Avon River towards the Stratford-on-Avon. The pub's picturesque waterside setting, proximity to the hospital and well-timed happy hour all combined to make it a popular watering hole for the staff of the Children's Hospital.

'Can you stay for a feed tonight?' Carrie asked as they pushed open the door and entered the pub.

Maia shook her head. 'I'm singing tonight. The band has a gig at the Cathedral Square Hotel,' she said as they ordered two bottles of cider.

Maia loved to sing. If she'd been good enough

to make a living out of it, she would have tried, but her father had convinced her to have a career as well and she'd discovered nursing, which she loved just as much. But she sang as often as she could with a jazz band.

The girls took their drinks out onto the deck that overlooked the Avon River. Willow trees lined the bank, their sweeping branches dipping into the calm waters. It was a pleasant spot on a summer's afternoon. They could watch the occasional punt taking tourists along the river or the university rowing crews on their afternoon trainings.

Today it was a rowing four that glided past as Maia asked, 'Are you still okay to come to the dressmaker with me next week?'

'Are you finally going to pick out the dresses?'

'No.' Maia laughed and sipped her cider. 'I'm hoping you'll do that.' Carrie was Maia's maid of honour and along with Maia's three younger sisters would form the bridal party. The wedding was only six weeks away. Maia needed to stop procrastinating and make some decisions. Todd had done most of the preparation work. Maia had given her opinion but she wasn't the one driving this.

'I'm surprised he hasn't given up on you,' Carrie said. 'You've made him wait for almost two years.'

'Maybe he thinks I'm worth it.' She grinned.

'I'm sure he does. But what do you think? Is he worth it?'

'He's a great guy, anybody would be lucky to have him. *I'm* lucky to have him,' she said but even she could hear the uncertain tone of her voice.

'You don't need to convince me,' Carrie replied.

Maia didn't answer; her mind was wandering, off on its own little tangent. They'd been engaged for eighteen months, since just before her dad had died. Was she lucky Todd was so patient or had she been secretly hoping that he'd get tired of waiting for her? Maia looked down the river as she pondered the question. The water was flat and green. A light breeze stirred the willow trees, making their leaves brush over the water. A rowing eight glided past, young, fit men wearing university colours disturbing the surface of the river as she stared off into the distance.

'My dad loved Todd. He became like the son he'd never had. He gave us his blessing before he died and you know how important that is to me,' she said, answering her own question. 'Family was everything to Dad.'

'I know that but are you sure you're marrying him because *you* want to, not just because your dad approved? Are you sure it's the right thing for you? Are you ready?'

She knew what Carrie was asking. She and Carrie had been friends for ever. They'd been friends before Maia's dad had got sick, before Maia had met Todd, before everything. They'd been friends before boyfriends, even, and Carrie had been there every step of the way. She knew which boys had been important, which one Maia had loved and which one had left her heartbroken.

Carrie knew her history with Henry. She knew that Henry had broken her heart—unintentionally, but it had been broken all the same. It had taken a long time for the cracks to heal and Maia knew they could easily be prised apart. But, despite heartache, life went on. Todd had filled a gap for her and somewhere along the way he'd helped her look to the future. A future that was different from what she had dreamed of and hoped for in some ways, but getting married was Maia's choice. She knew she'd been influenced by her father's thoughts and feelings, and by circumstances, but it didn't necessarily mean it was the wrong thing for her.

'It's a new year,' Maia said in reply. 'And my resolution was to look to the future and be happy with what I have.' Todd might not have been her first love but he would be a good husband. He was loyal, trustworthy, dependable and he adored her.

But, if she'd known the future was going to bring Henry back into her life, would she have made a different choice? It was too late to ask that question.

'Besides,' she continued, 'everything is booked—the cathedral, the reception venue, the cake, the photographer and the hairdresser.'

'It can always be un-booked.'

Maia wasn't so sure. 'We posted the invitations yesterday.'

The wedding was six weeks away. The sun kept rising and setting, the days kept turning over, and suddenly she was near the end of her engagement. This was it.

Maia closed her eyes as she started another song. It was one of her favourites, made famous by Ella Fitzgerald. She left the microphone fixed into the stand but steadied it with one hand as she swayed in time with the music. She'd chosen to wear a long, black dress tonight and it brushed her calves and ankles as she moved. It was cut low in the front and hugged her curves but a split up one leg to her thigh allowed for movement. Sequins scattered over the dress caught the light. There were more than a few men in the bar who were watching her with interest but, for the moment, she was oblivious to the attention as she let her mind drift.

Tonight the band was performing in the piano bar of the Cathedral Square Hotel in the city centre. This had become a semi-regular gig for her and the band. There were five of them tonight: the pianist, the bass player, the drummer, the trumpeter and her. The band had a different repertoire for the nights when she was unavailable due to nursing shifts and on those nights the pianist became the lead singer.

A spotlight was focused on her but she wasn't aware of it. When she sang she wasn't aware of anything except the music and the lyrics. It was one of the things she loved about singing.

It transported her to another world where she wasn't thinking about work or weddings or loss.

The spotlight highlighted Maia's exotic features. Her English and Maori heritage had blended together, giving her the best of both worlds. Her shape and colouring was courtesy of her Maori background on both sides of her family. Her round face, round cheeks, generous bust and generous hips, along with her masses of thick dark hair and brown eyes, were definitely Maori, as was her skin, with its hint of coffee. Her facial features were the image of her half-English mother, with the same almond-shaped dark eyes, finely arched brows and narrow nose.

She'd done her make-up tonight to suit the atmosphere of the piano bar. She'd painted her lips red and gone with dark, smoky eyes. She wasn't normally much of a make-up wearer—she was far too lazy to bother most days and she never wore make-up to work—but she made an exception on the nights when she performed with the band. She enjoyed the chance to get dressed up and performing on stage was all about playing a role and she was determined to do her part justice.

Tonight's performance was going smoothly. The crowd was reasonable; their first set had been well received and the applause was reassuring. Some nights Maia felt invisible on stage despite the spotlight.

She was pleased to have this gig tonight; it meant less time to think about Henry's reappearance. Despite her reassurances to Carrie, Henry's return had unsettled her more than she was prepared to admit. She had been twenty-two when they'd met, he'd been her first love and it seemed that neither her head nor her heart had forgotten him. But in a day or two she was sure she'd be fine. In a day or two she would have recovered from the shock of seeing him again.

She was halfway through a song, her eyes still closed, when she felt an odd stirring in the air as if someone had opened a window and let a breeze in. The breeze floated past her, caressing her skin and whispering in her ear. She opened her eyes and looked out into the crowd.

He stood by the bar on the far side of the room, watching her.

She watched him back. There weren't many things that could distract Maia when she was singing, but there was always one exception to any rule, and she knew this man was it.

He had showered and changed after work and he wore a black business shirt with the sleeves rolled up. Maia's eyes swept across his chest and followed the line of his arms before drifting down to his narrow hips which were encased in a pair of dark jeans. He had one hand hooked into the pocket of his jeans and in the other he held a glass of beer. He raised the glass towards her in a silent salute. Maia felt the breeze brush over her again and this time it whispered his name.

Henry.

Her breath caught in her throat as their eyes

locked and she lost her place in the song. Even at this distance she could see the intensity in his indigo eyes and feel the heat in his gaze. Warmth flooded through her, pooling in her belly, and she couldn't even begin to try to find the words to continue singing. She had been swaying to the music but now she was worried that her knees were going to give way beneath her. She gripped the microphone stand with both hands as she tried to keep herself upright. She turned her head to look at the pianist, breaking eye contact with Henry in the process. Sean, the pianist, mouthed the words to her and somehow she managed to pick up the pieces and finish the song with a breathless voice and her eyes tightly shut.

As the song wrapped she didn't give the band a chance to launch into the next one. The moment the music ended, she stepped away from the microphone and said, 'Can we take a short break, guys?'

'Is everything all right?' Sean asked.

Maia nodded. 'Everything's fine,' she lied.

Things were definitely not all right.

She didn't remember stepping off the stage or walking through the bar but she must have done so because now she was standing in front of Henry.

'Hello, Maia.' His British accent caressed her name and Maia's knees wobbled again. His voice was deep and gentle and his blue eyes were smiling.

Was it only today that he had come back into her life? It felt like he'd never left. It felt like everything that had happened since had been a dream, or perhaps she was dreaming now.

He took her hands and kissed her on the cheek. They were not in the hospital now; there were no concerns about protocol. She closed her eyes and held her breath as her limbs turned to liquid. This was definitely not a dream.

Her heart raced as his lips imprinted on her skin. What was it about him that could do this to her? How was it possible that a simple kiss on the cheek could leave her breathless and excited and make her feel as if she could melt away? As if she could dissolve in a pool of desire? One kiss from Henry and she could feel herself unfurling, coming back to life. She thought she had been doing okay but now she realised she'd been surviving, not living. She'd been getting through her days, but the days had had a dullness about them. One kiss from Henry and the colours began to return.

How could he affect her like this after all this time? How could she let him?

She stepped back as annoyance overrode pleasure and guilt replaced desire. She'd forgotten all about Todd. She found it irritating that Henry could return after three years and immediately influence her like this. But she wasn't sure who she was annoyed with—him or her.

She wouldn't give in. She wouldn't give him the satisfaction of knowing he still set her heart racing. It had taken her years to put her heart back together and she wasn't going to let one kiss reopen the scar where it had healed.

'What are you doing here?' she asked.

'I was on my way to my room and I thought I heard you singing. I thought I'd check.'

'You're staying here?'

He nodded. 'Just until I can find some decent short-term accommodation close to the hospital.' He pulled his room card out of his pocket. 'Have you got time for a drink? My shout.'

She shook her head. 'I'm working.'

'Just a quick one, for old times' sake. We've got some catching up to do.'

She looked into his indigo eyes and said, 'It's been three years, Henry. That's a lot of catching up.'

'Have dinner with me tomorrow, then.'

No. She couldn't do that, for so many reasons. She didn't trust herself. Or him. Her best defence was to stay as far away from him as possible, though that would be difficult, given they were working together. But she certainly didn't have to complicate things further by agreeing to have dinner with him. She glanced back over her shoulder. The stage had been abandoned. The band had taken advantage of her abrupt exit and were taking a break—surely one quick drink couldn't hurt? 'One drink.'

There was an empty table beside them. Henry pulled out a chair for her and she sat. It seemed she lacked the willpower to refuse his invitation. No, she admitted, if only to herself, she didn't lack the will power—she lacked the desire to walk away. She had never been able to resist him.

'What can I get you? A glass of Marlborough Sauvignon Blanc?'

'No. I don't drink wine if I'm singing.' There was always the risk that her sinuses would become congested. 'I'll have a vodka, lime and soda.'

Henry signalled to the waitress and ordered Maia's drink.

'How was San Francisco?' she asked, filling in the silence while she waited for her drink.

'Interesting. I really liked it.'

'You didn't want to stay?'

He shook his head. 'I left there a year ago. I've been in Tokyo for the last twelve months, studying the medical implications and response to tsunamis. It was time to come back and put what I've learnt about disaster management into practice.'

The waitress placed Maia's drink on the table. Condensation settled on the outside of the glass and Maia wiped it off with one finger as she thought about all the things that Henry would have seen and done over the past three years. The diamond in her engagement ring caught the light and Henry's eye as Maia ran her finger over the glass. He reached for her hand and just the barest touch of his fingers on her skin made her catch her breath. While she was connected to him she felt like she ceased to exist.

As if nothing else mattered but the two of them. As if they were one.

She knew he shouldn't have this effect on her still. Three years was a long time. It should have given her time to forget. Time had moved on. *She* had moved on. But her body didn't seem to have received the same message.

His thumb rested in her palm as he turned her hand, and the solitaire diamond sparkled. 'You're engaged?'

She nodded. She'd taken it off her necklace and had slipped it back onto her finger as she was getting dressed tonight.

'Anyone I know?'

'Not really.' The rapid beating of her heart made her voice sound breathless.

'What does that mean?'

'You saw him today but there was no time to introduce you.' There'd been no reason to introduce them either but Maia knew she hadn't wanted to.

'The paramedic who brought Adam in?'

It seemed he had noticed Todd's hand on her shoulder. Noticed and remembered. Maia nodded.

'When is the wedding?'

'Six weeks.'

Henry sat back in his seat and let go of her hand. She noticed he hadn't congratulated her. What did that mean?

Probably nothing. She couldn't afford to read anything into the silence. It wasn't her place to speculate about his thoughts.

'Timing was never one of our strong points,' he said.

She studied his expression but it was difficult to read in the dim lights of the bar. Did he have regrets too?

Maia shook her head. 'No, it wasn't.' His regrets were no longer her concern. They couldn't be. Her life had changed when her father had died and it was naive to think things could ever go back to the way they were. Their lives hadn't fitted together three years ago; it was unlikely they would fit together any better now. Nothing he'd said made her think his priorities had changed.

'So things have worked out well for you?' he asked. 'You're happy?'

'Of course.' She was, wasn't she? She had nothing to be unhappy about. She was healthy, she loved her job, she had family, friends and a fiancé who loved her.

She didn't want to think about why Todd was last on her list. Was that where he fitted in her life?

She should be happy. There was no reason not to be yet she knew she was lying. If she was happy why was she sitting here imagining what her life would have been like now if Henry had never left? Or if she'd gone with him? But that had never been seriously discussed.

They'd known at the beginning that their relationship would have an end. Henry's plans had already been in place. He'd been in Christchurch for a limited time, she'd known the date he was leaving and she had known he wouldn't take her with him. He travelled alone. That was his choice and, while she didn't like it, she'd had to accept it. Then, just weeks after his departure, her dad had suffered his first stroke and Maia had known then she would have chosen to stay. But it had been tough, really tough, and in the end she had lost both her father and Henry.

'Things have worked out differently to what I expected but that's life, isn't it?' she said. 'Things change and you have to change with them.'

She could see the band members making their way back onto the stage. She pushed her chair back and stood. 'I have to go.'

Henry got up too and came to her side. 'I'll see you soon,' he said as he leant forward and kissed her cheek a second time, making her stomach flutter.

Oh, God, how was she going to handle this? How on earth had she thought she was over him? Just one kiss and she could feel herself falling again. She needed to get out of here.

Somehow Maia managed to get through two more songs. Henry had stayed for both before leaving the room. She doubted he'd return to the piano bar tonight but she didn't want to hang around to find out. She told the band she wasn't feeling well and made an early exit. An exit that felt very much like an escape.

The hotel doorman hailed her a taxi and she spent the ride home thinking about Henry. She thought she had managed to put him out of her mind. She would have thought three years was long enough to stop thinking about him and it should have been long enough for her body to forget him. But her reaction tonight proved that wasn't the case. Her body definitely hadn't got the message that three years had passed—her body had sprung to life as if it had been dormant these past few years.

Did her body have a memory all of its own? A memory that was independent of her brain?

She had no complaints about her sex life with Todd, it was pleasantly satisfying. But there was no denying that sex with Henry had been incredible. Those memories must have been repressed but not forgotten for them to return to the forefront of her mind so quickly.

Sex with Henry had been amazing. It had been passionate, all-consuming, powerful and never routine. Sex with Henry had been nothing like she'd ever experienced before or after. He could almost bring her to orgasm with just one look, one touch, one well-placed kiss. And now he was back.

Why now? Why not six months ago? Or never. It was too late now.

Maia sighed. There was no point dwelling on missed opportunities. There were things she was never going to get to do and there was no point looking backward. Life had other plans for her.

\* \* \*

'Experts are predicting that last week's quake was just a precursor to a more powerful and potentially devastating one. Obviously, they can't predict when but we need to be prepared and put plans in place. It's a case of *when*, not if, as far as the experts are concerned.'

Maia and most of the ED staff were listening to Henry as he spoke about disaster management in his smooth British accent.

'A mass casualty situation is something that would stretch our hospital, and others, in terms of managing the number of injured—for example, a major earthquake. Canterbury Children's already has good systems in place. The emergency department staff is exceptionally well-trained, but in the event of a major disaster we would need to call in additional staff from other areas of the hospital and we would benefit from improving some of our systems to assist those staff who are unfamiliar with the ED environment. The easier we can make it for them to slot into our workplace, the more efficient and effective we will be, which will mean lives saved.

'Our triage nurses will be stationed at the main entrances with security and they will be responsible for deciding which casualties come into the hospital and which ones are sent elsewhere.'

He had been back for ten days and Maia was coping. Just. She had found avoidance the easiest way of managing so far but this was an important presentation she hadn't wanted to miss.

He was wearing a set of dark blue surgical scrubs, the ones that made his indigo eyes look even darker than usual, and Maia was hard pressed to recall anyone who looked better in a pair of unflattering scrubs than Henry. The scrubs looked as if they'd been tailor-made for his broad chest and the pants hugged his hips and the rounded cheeks of his bottom.

'Internally we create teams of ED staff supported by staff from other wards or departments. Ideally we would have an ED doc, ED nurse, anaesthetist and a second nurse in each team. I would suggest using medical or nursing students to act as runners and they can also assist with making up packs—for example, assembling hyperkalaemia packs if we are expecting multiple crush injuries. Everyone will be given a job card which will explain who they report to. The ward doctor will report to the ED doctor in their team, the ED doctor reports to the ED doctor in charge and so on.

'We are also going to implement a mass casualty box,' he said as he lifted a large red box, the size of an archive box, onto the table in front of him. Maia watched his biceps bulge as he hefted the carton. He really was very sexy in a British way. He had a cool, calm exterior but she knew the passionate nature that hid beneath that collected facade. She knew he kept a tight rein on his emotions and he was extremely strong-willed but once she'd been allowed to scratch the surface his true character had been revealed—

passionate, intense and heartbreakingly gorgeous. He really was divine.

'It contains all the patient identification paraphernalia you might need, including "unknown patient" labels, as it's very likely you will get patients who have not been formally identified.' Henry pulled various documents out of the box as he spoke. 'There are wrist bands, paper-based ED charts, lab forms, X-ray forms as well as patient-tracking forms and simple instruction cards. Brenda and I would like you all to familiarise yourselves with the contents of this box.

'We'll make use of social workers to act as patient liaisons. The hospital has HR personnel trained in media liaison—these professionals will keep the media and the families informed and this will free up all ED staff to do their jobs without interruptions.

'One major change to procedure that we are planning on implementing is that patients who leave ED, say for X-ray, don't come back but go directly to a ward or Theatre. The surgical team can decide that in radiology but this will help to keep the ED turning over and reduce congestion and hopefully waiting times.

'We're hopeful that these changes will make it easier for the ED staff to do their jobs and to assist staff from other departments to help us without complicating process and treatment. We want to streamline triage with the intention of saving as many lives as possible in the event of a mass casualty.'

Henry took questions at the end of his discussion but as the staff milled around him Maia chose to escape outside. His talk had been excellent, but she needed to put some distance between him and her wayward thoughts before she lost control. His focus was still very clearly on disaster management, on emergency medicine, on saving the world. His priorities hadn't changed and she would do well to remember that.

Maia lay on the grass that ran along the northern side of the emergency department. She was waiting for Carrie, who was finishing off some administrative work for Brenda, but the weather was too nice to waste by waiting inside. It was a glorious summer's afternoon and Maia figured she might as well work on her tan while she killed time. Her eyes were closed, her face turned up to the sun as she let it warm her skin. A shadow passed over her and she opened her eyes to find Henry standing in front of her.

'I brought you a coffee,' he said as he held it out to her.

Maia sat up, cross-legged, on the grass. 'How did you know I was here?'

'I saw you as I was going to buy some lunch. Sugar?' he asked.

'Thank you.'

He took a sachet and stirring stick out of the pocket on the front of his surgical shirt and held them out to her as he lowered himself onto the ground beside her. She removed the lid from her cup and emptied the sugar into her drink.

He stretched out on the grass, resting back on his elbows, and groaned.

Maia smiled. 'You sound exhausted.'

'Public speaking *is* exhausting.'

She stirred the sugar into her coffee as she looked at Henry. His dark blue eyes seemed violet. They were stunning and she felt the now familiar increase in her heart rate and body temperature that occurred whenever he was nearby. But she decided she could enjoy his company for a few minutes; after all, he'd sought her out and there was no one around to wonder about the blush that stained her cheeks.

'Poor you.' She laughed. 'I suppose you've got to go back inside after lunch and save more lives on top of everything else.'

'Of course, don't you?'

'Nope, I've got the day off.'

'Did you come in just to listen to me?'

'I did.'

'I'm flattered.'

'Don't be,' she teased him. 'I have to get my

continuing professional development points up but, if it makes you feel better, I thought it was worthwhile.'

'Thank you. Have you got something nice planned for your afternoon?'

'I'm waiting for Carrie; we're going shopping,' she said.

'Really? That's what you're doing on your day off? The Maia I remember always hated shopping.'

'I still do, but I'm afraid I'm on a deadline.' She was running out of time.

'Wedding shopping?'

Maia nodded. She was supposed to be going to look at dresses with Carrie. They needed to choose bridesmaids' dresses and she still hadn't done anything about her own dress. Or the flowers.

'How long to go now, four weeks?'

'Four and a half.'

'You're young to be getting married—bucking the trend.'

'I'm twenty-five, it's not that young,' she said. 'My mum was married when she was nineteen and Todd is thirty-two.'

'My age.'

She wondered if Henry thought that was too young also. Probably. She knew how he felt about commitment and it didn't seem as if he'd changed his mind in the past three years.

'We've been engaged for eighteen months,' she added.

'Since your dad died?'

'Yes. Todd nursed my dad, that's how we met.'

Henry frowned. 'Isn't he a paramedic?'

'He is now. He was a nurse when we met but he was studying to become a paramedic and he was working in home care. He was one of the nurses who looked after Dad so that Dad could stay home like he wanted. My father lost the power of speech with his stroke but Todd was able to understand him. He and Dad got along exceptionally well, so after the first couple of months Todd was the nurse who came most often and between the two of us and Mum we nursed Dad.'

Which meant Maia had spent hours sitting by her dad's bed and hours talking to Todd. Todd hadn't needed to spend as much time as he had at their house, he didn't get paid for a lot of it, and Maia knew that he'd chosen to spend time at their house as a way of spending time with her. That had been flattering and she knew she'd encouraged it. The attention had helped divert her mind from a host of other things including her father's condition and Henry's absence.

She and Todd had talked about lots of things: their work, their hobbies, their families and their plans. All those shared stories had bonded them until it had seemed like a natural progression to spend their free time together too.

'Todd asked Dad for his permission to marry me just a few weeks before Dad suffered his second stroke. That was eighteen months ago.'

Todd had helped her gradually to let go of the idea of Henry, and even though Henry was back now she had to remember he wasn't part of her life. She had a new life. With Todd. A life she couldn't have with Henry.

Henry was the past. He'd left her once before and she knew he would leave again. She could feel it in the air around him. That restlessness, that distance. Just like she could feel the attraction. But she knew that his restlessness was still too strong a force to overcome with chemistry. He wouldn't choose to stay and she craved stability. She needed that commitment; she needed to know that she could depend on someone.

Maia had been there when Todd had spoken to her father. She'd seen her father's reaction, seen the delight in his eyes, and knowing that was the last thing that had made him truly happy before he'd died meant that she had accepted Todd's proposal. She knew he was pleased she was getting the security she wanted. Maia felt like it had been her father's dying wish that she and Todd marry. How could she do otherwise?

* * *

Maia had a guarded look in her eyes and Henry knew she wasn't telling him the full story. What had happened to her to put that look there? She was older, maybe wiser, but he knew she'd been hurt. Maybe her dad's premature death had made her wary or maybe she had reserved that look just for him.

His pager beeped, calling him back to the ED. He said goodbye to Maia and left her in the sunshine. He had to walk away. She was getting what she always wanted—security and commitment—and Henry imagined that after her father's death that was possibly even more important.

There was nothing for him here. Nothing for her either. It didn't matter how he felt—it didn't matter that he was still attracted to her or that there was still chemistry between them. It was clear that Maia had moved on. She was about to be married. Which was probably a good thing. His circumstances hadn't changed. He wouldn't commit and it was obvious that was still what Maia wanted.

He could ignore the stirrings of desire. He had walked away before. It had turned out to be one of the hardest things he'd ever done but that had been his choice and it would be his choice again. When he'd met Maia he'd been alone for years but leaving her behind had made him lonely. It had been a bizarre, unexpected feeling but his circumstances hadn't changed in the past three years. He still wasn't willing to commit to a place or a person. He still had nothing to offer her and he knew he would walk away again. Love was too big a risk. Family was everything to her, a concept he understood but no longer had time for.

He would be here for a while and he'd move on again. Alone. It was better that way. Safer.

He and Maia could both have what they wanted—but not together.

# CHAPTER FOUR

'WHAT ABOUT THIS?' Carrie asked as she flicked through racks of rainbow-coloured dresses. They were surrounded by metres and metres of chiffon, silk and lace but Maia was not feeling particularly enthused. She really didn't mind what the girls wore and choosing something that would suit them all was proving to be a nightmare. Carrie was short, blonde and fair skinned. Maia's sisters were all dark, like her, in varying proportions. Pippi was tall and thin; she was almost sixteen and hadn't started to spread through the hips yet, like eighteen-year-old Ariana. At twenty, Lani, the second eldest, was big breasted but short. They had to find something that would suit three different body shapes and Maia didn't see why it had to be her decision.

'Maybe we should choose a colour and a fabric but have two different styles,' Carrie suggested. 'Pippi and I could wear the same dress and Lani and Ariana could wear something else but in the same colour and fabric?'

Maia rifled through the racks as she tried to drum up some enthusiasm. 'But what colour?' In her opinion that was almost the hardest decision. Black wouldn't be flattering on her sisters, and white wasn't a good colour on Carrie. Red would suit her sisters but wash Carrie out. Bright blue looked lovely on all of them but Maia couldn't imagine having her bridesmaids in a bright colour.

'How about green?' Carrie was holding out two different dresses in the same pale mint green. It was a pretty colour and probably would suit all the girls but Maia was over it.

She groaned and collapsed onto the sofa in the shop window. She could feel the beginnings of a headache. Maybe it would be best to get this sorted out quickly and then Carrie might let her out of the shop. 'You decide,' she said. She almost said, *I don't care anymore*, but stopped just in time. A comment like that would only invite more questions from Carrie and Maia was tired of thinking.

She felt like she was making decisions for someone else. Last night she and Todd had gone to dinner at the hotel where they had booked their reception. She'd wanted to cancel the reservation, to claim exhaustion, but guilt had made her keep to the plan. It wasn't Todd's fault that she was at sixes and sevens. It wasn't his fault that she felt like it was impossible to think straight, let alone make a decision. They had finalised the menu and the drinks, and the position of the dance floor and the table for the wedding cake, but this morning Maia couldn't remember what any of the decisions had been.

Her brain was completely addled and today was only making it worse. Today was a kaleidoscope of decisions about shoes, dresses, makeup and flowers. For someone who didn't love shopping *or* making decisions that weren't work related, it was proving to be a little overwhelming.

'Why are you so grumpy?' Carrie asked as she handed the dresses to the sales assistant and sent her off to find out what other styles and sizes were available in that colour. 'Is it Henry?'

'Henry? What does he have to do with anything?'

'I don't know. That's why I'm asking.'

'It's nothing to do with Henry. That was all over long before I met Todd.'

'Yes, I know, but now he's back. Are you telling me that hasn't changed things? Do you still have feelings for him?'

'I've moved on. We both have.' But even as she said the words a part of her wished things were different. 'I'm sure this is just a case of pre-wedding jitters.'

'Also known as cold feet.'

'Which is perfectly normal, everyone says so. Everything will be fine once we're married.'

Carrie was looking at her closely and Maia waited for her to say more but the return of the sales assistant interrupted their conversation. She had her arms full of dresses and she hung them on an empty clothes rack for Carrie to sort through. Maia waited as Carrie separated a couple of possibilities and the sales assistant stripped two store mannequins and redressed them with Carrie's choices.

Carrie stood back and studied the dresses while she spoke to Maia. 'Okay, I'll choose for the bridesmaids, but *you* have to choose your wedding dress.'

They had started off the afternoon looking at wedding gowns but Maia had tired of that quickly too. There had been a couple she'd liked—one was strapless with a heavily beaded bodice and full skirt, and the other was a far more simple, bias-cut satin that draped over her hips and had wide, simple straps that crossed her chest and showed off her shoulders. But they'd been so different she hadn't been able to choose between them so she'd given up.

'Stop worrying,' she told Carrie. 'Everything will be fine.'

'I'm your maid of honour—making sure you are doing the right thing is part of my job description.' She swapped one of the dresses on the mannequin for another as she continued. 'Wedding dresses are a bit like men. You don't need more than one. You can like different things about different wedding dresses, or men, but in the end you only need one wedding dress and you only need one man. I can't choose your wedding dress for you. Only you can do that. And only you can choose the right man. No one else can do that for you either. You just have to choose the man who's best for you. Not the one who can't live without you but the one who *you* can't live without.'

'It's all good,' Maia said. She was convinced that once she and Todd were husband and wife she would settle down. Once that day was over and the decision was final, she'd be happy. Her life, their life, would be smooth sailing; Todd would make sure of it. He would look after her. She loved Todd. He was kind and loyal; he loved her family. It didn't matter that she'd loved Henry first. Todd's priorities—work, her and family—were the same as hers. That was important. 'I know what you're thinking—that Henry's return has unsettled me—but that's not the case. Henry wasn't the right man for me.'

'Why? Because he left?'

'No.' Maia shook her head, trying to convince herself that she spoke the truth. 'I want a family. I want to be settled and I want someone I can depend on, someone I know will be there for me. Henry doesn't want a family; he doesn't want to settle down. He wants to save the world, one disaster at a time. That's his priority, that's his choice, and it was never going to include me. I've made my choice. I'm marrying Todd.'

But was Todd really the one she couldn't live without?

\* \* \*

Maia was finding it difficult to concentrate. She had come to the Queen Elizabeth Hospital for a half-day seminar on advances in emergency medicine and this session was a discussion on latest practice in paediatric anaesthesia. The sessions had been good so far and she was looking forward to this one, the final one of the day. She was expecting it to be both informative and interesting but she was finding it hard to focus because in the darkened theatre, in the seat beside her, with his thigh brushing hers, sat Henry.

The lights had been dimmed and Maia was aware of the slides changing as the speaker went through her presentation. But she was more aware of the length of Henry's thigh in his stone-coloured chinos, the slight jiggle of his leg as he listened and the smell of his aftershave. The scent of grapefruit and cedar wafted over her and she could feel his body heat radiating from his arm where it rested next to hers on the arm of his seat.

Maia had to tuck her hands between her thighs so she didn't reach out and touch him. She could hear him breathing. She counted his breaths, trying to stop herself from thinking about touching him, but then she forgot to listen to the lecturer.

Occasionally Henry would lean towards her and whisper a comment to her about the lecture content. His breath was warm and soft on her cheek and his aftershave mesmerised her and pulled her in closer. She could feel herself leaning towards him until their upper arms touched, startling her and making her shift away. She wanted to touch him, she wanted to feel him. She wanted to rest her hand on his thigh. She wanted to sit in the dark and hold his hand. But she couldn't do any of those things.

Fifteen minutes into the presentation, Henry slouched in his seat, his knees relaxed and his left thigh bumped into hers. She was convinced she could feel his firm, muscular thigh even through the thin layers of their clothing. She could definitely feel the heat radiating from his skin. She pressed her knees together primly, trying to avoid temptation. But it was impossible to maintain that uptight posture, it was impossible to maintain that distance, and eventually, when it all got too much, she decided she would excuse herself to go to the bathroom and when she came back she would sit somewhere else. Somewhere that wasn't next to Henry.

She was about to stand up and sneak out when the lecturer finished her presentation and the lights came up ready for question time. She couldn't sneak out now. She would have to sit and wait.

She sat as still as possible and fought off the waves of guilt. She hadn't done anything, and didn't intend to, but knowing that didn't stop the desire. She could feel Henry calling for her, his body speaking to hers in their own silent language. Her skin longed to feel his touch, her lips longed to taste him, her heart wanted to beat in time with his. She wanted to breathe his scent and see his indigo eyes darken with longing for her and hear him call out her name.

But it couldn't be. She had promised her heart and her body to someone else.

Surely this desire would fade once she got used to having Henry back in Christchurch? Surely it was just the unexpectedness and the excitement of the situation that made her feel this way? Surely this spark of desire, this attraction, this sense of longing, would diminish with time?

Maybe once she was married she would be able to put him behind her once and for all. Surely that commitment to Todd would put an end to her inappropriate thoughts about Henry? That was how she would handle this. She could put this extra energy that Henry seemed to instil in her to good use—she could put this energy into planning the final details of her wedding. And she might as well start now. Once this seminar was over she would go to the boutique and make a final decision about her wedding dress.

She only had four weeks to go. It was time to focus on what was important, on her future with Todd. Henry belonged in the past.

Finally question time was finished and the morning was over and she could escape. She stood up and collected her bag and her water bottle.

'Are you going back to the Children's?' Henry asked as he followed her out of the lecture theatre.

Maia shook her head. 'This is a professional development day for me. I'm not rostered on to work.'

'I have to be back at two, but if you've got time how about I shout you a burger at the Stratford?'

In her head she'd already planned her exit strategy. Having lunch together wasn't part of it. Spending more time with him wasn't going to help her resist temptation. 'I shouldn't,' she replied.

'It's just a burger, Maia, I'm not asking you to run away with me.'

How did he always know what she was thinking, even when her thoughts were completely inappropriate? She almost wished he *would* ask her to run away with him.

No, not that exactly; that would involve her making a conscious decision. She wished he would steal her away and solve her dilemma without her having to decide anything.

She hesitated as right and wrong argued with each other, as suitable and unsuitable behaviours clashed, and as desire, want and need fought with loyalty in her mind.

Desire, want and need won.

It was an absolutely glorious summer's day. There wasn't a cloud in the sky, the sun was shining and it warmed her skin. There was a light breeze but it wasn't enough to take the warmth out of the sun. To spend a little time outside after being cooped up in the darkness of the lecture theatre would be wonderful and Maia could think of nothing nicer than to sit on the deck overlooking the river and share a meal with Henry. The boutique would still be there after lunch. What could be the harm in sharing an innocent bite to eat?

'Of course.' She nodded. 'Just a burger. That sounds lovely,' she said, accepting his invitation.

They strolled together along the footpath, two friends going to grab some lunch. Only she couldn't pretend that was all it was. As far as she knew friends weren't so aware of each other. She could feel the air buzzing. They weren't touching but she could feel the pull of electricity that hummed between them and she was aware of every movement he made. They walked in time, falling into old patterns and rhythms, but she made sure to keep some distance between them. She couldn't afford to touch him.

They passed behind the Cathedral Square Hotel on their way to the square. 'Are you singing here on the weekend?' he asked.

Maia nodded. 'Saturday night.'

'Maybe I'll come and listen again.'

'Are you still staying in the hotel?' Henry had

been back in town for almost two weeks and she'd assumed he would have found other accommodation by now even if it was just a serviced apartment.

'I haven't had time to view anything yet but the estate agent has lined up a few possibilities for me that I'll look at on Saturday. Hopefully by this time next week I'll be sorted,' he said. 'While I don't mind the on-site restaurant, bar and laundry service at the hotel, I'd like my own space—but finding something close to the hospital isn't easy, apparently.'

'Have you checked the hospital noticeboards?' she asked. 'Someone might be looking for a flatmate.'

'I haven't,' Henry admitted as they rounded the corner of the hotel and the Christchurch Cathedral came into view. 'I'm a bit past sharing digs. I was thinking more along the lines of a serviced apartment.'

As always the cathedral drew Maia's attention. It was a gorgeous building, a landmark in the centre of the city, and it dominated the square and never failed to catch her eye. She looked up to the very top of the silver spire. If she had been alone she would have detoured inside to light a candle for her dad but she didn't want to delay Henry. She didn't want to miss her opportunity to have lunch with him. She'd return later instead on her way back to the dress shop.

A flock of pigeons roosted on the cathedral roof. They were a permanent fixture, the bane of the church's existence, and while Maia watched them they all suddenly took to the sky. En masse they flew east away from the city and towards the coast. Maia frowned and wondered what had spooked them. She searched the sky for the telltale shadow of a falcon but the sky remained blue and clear and the air was still and eerily quiet. There was no longer even a whisper of a breeze. Something was wrong but she could see no signs and she shivered as a feeling of apprehension ran down her spine. She looked around but could see nothing.

Henry had walked ahead of her and was waiting in the square. She tried to shake off the foreboding of impending doom as she hurried to catch up but as she took two quick steps her right knee gave way underneath her. She righted her balance, assuming she must have trodden on an uneven bit of footpath, but then she heard the rumbling. It vibrated through the ground beneath her and she realised she hadn't missed her step or caught her foot but rather the earth was moving.

The footpath rose and fell in front of her, cracking along its length as she struggled to keep her feet. The ground shook violently and the road beside her undulated as if it was liquid, rolling away from her like a wave going out to sea, leaving behind volcanic peaks of bitumen, broken pipes and muddy craters. Maia watched in silent horror too terrified to make a sound, as the earth cracked open and enormous dust clouds rose into the air as buildings crumbled and collapsed around the square like decks of cards.

This was the one they'd been warned about. This was the earthquake the experts had predicted.

As Maia listened to the earth groan, and watched it heave as if it was alive and in pain, she wondered why they hadn't all left Christchurch long before. Although she knew the answer to that question—no one ever really expected this to happen. The human mind could not comprehend disasters on this scale.

But now it was here. The one they'd been dreading but couldn't possibly have imagined.

The writhing and screaming of the earth was accompanied by other sounds: the crash of breaking glass and the thump of falling masonry as concrete collapsed and bricks and windows fell into the street; the loud blaring of car alarms and the strident blast of car horns. Maia heard metal being crushed as cars collided and above it all she could hear the high-pitched shriek of twisting steel as some of the buildings tried futilely to resist the power of the quake.

The ground bucked and heaved under her, making it impossible to stay on her feet. The rumbling increased in volume; it sounded as if a jumbo jet was going to land in the middle of the city. Maia knew that was impossible, she knew it was an earthquake, but she couldn't stop herself from looking up to the sky.

Above her the green, copper-plated roof of the cathedral bell tower was swaying violently and the silver spire which normally pointed up to the heavens was arcing like a pendulum. The earth continued to shudder and Maia watched in disbelief as stones began to plummet from the walls of the cathedral and the top half of the bell tower began to collapse.

It was falling.

It was falling and it was going to come crashing down right where she stood on wobbly legs but she couldn't make her legs move. She had no control over her muscles, her brain or her body. Her mind had shut down and all she could do was stand and watch as the bell tower and its silver spire fell towards her.

# CHAPTER FIVE

'*MAIA! MAIA!*'

One moment she'd been frozen to the spot, staring death in the face, waiting for the inevitable. The next she was lying on the ground in a cloud of dust. But the ground was soft. She was in Henry's arms, lying on his chest, metres from where she'd been standing seconds before. As the dust settled, the extent of the damage revealed itself.

The silver spire had crashed to the ground and was resting on the cathedral steps. The pavers where she had been standing were buried under blocks of stone and the green copper plating from the top section of the tower glowed in their midst.

Her heart thudded behind her ribs as adrenalin flowed through her veins.

'Are you okay?' Henry's words were soft in her ear.

She coughed and sat up. She was shaking violently and the only thing keeping her in a semi-upright position was Henry. His arms were still wrapped around her, holding her close, keeping her safe.

'I think so.' Her voice wobbled but she wasn't hurt. Henry had saved her life.

'Can you stand?' he asked.

Maia had no idea. There was only one way to find out.

'I think so,' she repeated.

The earth was still shaking as Henry helped her to her feet. Standing was better; she'd felt vulnerable and exposed while lying on the ground even though she'd been with Henry. It would have been impossible to run if need be while they'd both been lying down.

Her legs took her weight but she didn't let

go of Henry. She didn't think she could. She clung to him like a lone survivor to a life raft in a stormy sea and watched as Mother Nature continued to wreak havoc around them.

Across the square buildings continued to succumb to the force of nature as their facades separated from the rest of the structure and toppled into the street, burying sidewalks, parked cars and people.

The situation was horrifying and almost impossible to comprehend. They were in the middle of the city. It was lunchtime on a weekday. These buildings were shops and offices, cafés and churches. These buildings were filled with people.

One of the Christchurch trams had come to a stop alongside them. The tram tracks had become warped and twisted strips of metal, going nowhere. Tourists piled out of the tram, ejected into the centre of the chaos, where they stood, dazed and confused. People ran from the cathedral, running for their lives, only to come to a stop in the square. They had nowhere else to go.

The earthquake wasn't finished with the cathedral yet and Maia watched on in horror as the slate roof on the north-west corner of the building fell into the cathedral itself. Her knees buckled again. It felt like she was on a suspension bridge and someone was making the bridge wobble. She clung tighter to Henry to stop herself from falling. To her left a cloud of dust billowed up into the air and she buried her face in Henry's shoulder as the roof of the Press Building, on the edge of Cathedral Square, caved in.

Finally the world stopped moving. The ground stopped oscillating and the city stopped shaking. Maia found the sudden stillness and the quiet unnerving, almost as unnerving as the quake itself.

'Maia? Look at me.' Henry put two fingers under her chin and gently tipped her head up. 'Are you all right?' He brushed strands of her dark hair from her cheek and searched her face for an answer.

She nodded. She'd have some bruises tomorrow but otherwise she was unhurt.

The quake had probably lasted less than a minute but the damage was immense, incredible, unbelievable. There was no traffic noise. Everything had ground to a halt. There were only two sounds now, car alarms and people. She could hear people crying, people calling out, people dying. She could hear the awful sounds of things that should never happen.

Maia stayed in Henry's embrace and from there she was brave enough to look around.

The air was thick with dust. She could taste it. Her lips and throat were coated with it and it made her eyes itch but despite her watery eyes she could still see the carnage around them.

The dust obscured some of the drama and the damage but wasn't dense enough to hide the horror completely. Where city buildings had once stood was now nothing but rubble. Some of the buildings had collapsed in on themselves, others had fallen sideways onto neighbouring buildings or into the roads. Power lines and poles had come down and traffic lights were out. Cars had toppled into massive craters or had been crushed underneath ruined buildings.

The city of Christchurch was unrecognisable.

She hugged Henry tight, clinging to him, needing the reassurance that she could only get from touching another living soul. All around them people had lost their footing and had fallen to the ground. To her right she could see someone buried under a pile of debris but she instinctively knew there was nothing they could do to help save them—they were already too late. And that was the worst thing. In a disaster of this scale, knowing that there would be people for whom they could do nothing, that there were people who were beyond help, people who could not be saved, was almost more than she could bear.

And then people started to move. Some people wandered aimlessly, shocked and disorientated; some were on their phones, others were already dragging people from the wreckage. In the distance she could hear the sirens of the emergency vehicles as they began to respond to the crisis. The square and the surrounding streets looked like a war zone but people's responses were strangely orderly. There was no running, no mass panic. It was almost as if they had been through this before but Maia knew that wasn't the case. Christchurch hadn't experienced anything on this scale in her lifetime.

'Maia?' Henry's voice brought her back. 'Are you sure you're okay? We need to help.'

An elderly lady lay on the ground near Henry and Maia. A younger woman crouched at her side. The old lady was pale and trembling and the younger one looked up at Henry with tears in her eyes. 'Please, can you help us? I can't get my mother up.'

Henry went to her and Maia went with him, focusing her attention on the two women.

'Don't move her,' Henry said to the younger woman as he squatted down on the paving. The old lady's right leg lay at an unnatural angle and appeared shorter than the other. 'She's fractured her hip,' he told the daughter. The woman was wearing a summer dress and sensible shoes. Henry put his fingers on the inside of her ankle, feeling for a pulse. The woman's daughter frowned and looked at Maia, obviously wondering what Henry was doing.

'It's all right,' Maia told her. 'He's a doctor.'

'My name is Henry.' He was talking to the old lady. 'Do you know where you are?'

'No.'

Maia could see the confusion in the old woman's eyes.

'Is she normally alert?' Henry asked the daughter. 'She doesn't have memory loss or dementia?'

'No, she's perfectly normal. Why, what's the matter?' Maia could hear the tears in the daughter's voice.

'She could have hit her head when she fell,' Henry explained. 'Does she have any significant medical conditions?'

The daughter shook her head in reply.

'How old is she?'

'Eighty-one.'

Maia pulled out her phone and dialled 111 to call an ambulance as Henry continued to check the woman. Maia knew it was more than likely that all the ambulances would already be on the road but she needed to notify someone about the situation. Someone needed to be coordinating the trucks.

'Can you move your fingers?' Henry was asking.

Maia watched as the woman wriggled her fingers. That was a good sign.

The emergency operator patched Maia through to the ambulance call centre and she gave their location and as many details about the woman as she could. 'An eighty-one-year-old woman, probable fractured NOF, concussion, possible head and neck injuries.'

She pressed 'end' on her phone and spoke to the woman's daughter. 'An ambulance has been dispatched. They know you're here but I can't tell you how long they will be.'

Maia could hear people calling for help all around them. People called from the ruined buildings and they called from the streets, wanting assistance to rescue the survivors trapped inside the damaged structures.

Henry stood up, the desperate pleas for assistance galvanising him into action. 'I'm sorry,' he said. 'There isn't anything else we can do for her here. You'll have to wait for the ambulance. We need to go; other people need our help too.'

He was right. People had been killed—Maia could see more than one body. Those deaths were tragic but there wasn't anything they could do about them. It sounded harsh but it was the reality. She'd recovered from her initial dismay;

there were others who they could help, others who needed their help.

They walked down the buckled road, dodging the detritus of the quake. The street was a mess of potholes and cracks. The surface of the road was strewn with lumps of masonry, twisted signs and fallen light posts. Several water mains had ruptured and the road and the footpaths were flooded with muddy water and filth. On the street corner a couple of old, pre–World War II buildings had collapsed. Bricks and chunks of concrete from the facades had fallen onto parked cars, partially crushing some. The driver's door of the car nearest to Maia was open. It jutted into the roadway and a woman lay in the middle of the street. A chunk of masonry and a child's dummy lay beside each other near her right hand. Maia couldn't tell if she was alive or dead but as she crossed the street the woman's eyes opened.

She sat up as Maia and Henry approached and Maia could see she was bleeding from a cut on her head. The left side of her face was covered in a gruesome, bloody stain, as if someone had tipped a tin of dark red paint over her. She was struggling to her feet. Henry took her hand and helped her up. Her blue eyes were wild as she scanned her surroundings, as if she couldn't quite understand what she was seeing.

And then she started screaming and staggered towards the partially crushed car. Her blue eyes were wilder still as she turned to Henry and clutched his arm. 'My husband and daughter are in that car.'

Henry looked at Maia. His eyes were dark. He looked worried. 'Wait here,' he said as he gently disengaged her hand from his arm. 'I'll see what I can do.'

But she wasn't listening. 'That's my family,' she said as she took another step towards the car and this time it was Henry's turn to hold on to her.

He held her by her elbow, forcing her to stop, forcing her to look at him. 'Your family will need a doctor.' He spoke slowly and deliberately, maintaining eye contact, and his voice was quiet and calm. 'I'm a doctor. Let me help you.'

Maia wondered how many more times he would say that today. She wondered what he would be able to do, but it seemed that people trusted doctors. They were prepared to believe anything he told them.

'Maia will look after you and I will look after your family,' he continued.

He nodded ever so slightly to Maia. She knew what he wanted. What he needed. He needed her to take care of this woman. She looked ready to collapse. Even without the head injury, the stress and anxiety were going to make her a liability. She was going to be more of a hindrance than a help. Henry needed her out of the way.

But Maia was worried about Henry. The situation was confronting. There wasn't much left of the car. Surely this tragedy would bring back heart-rending memories for him? He wasn't an impassive, unaffected bystander; the situation was likely to feel very personal. How would he cope? How could she help him?

'Are you sure you want to do this?' she asked.

'This is what I've trained for. It's my way of making a difference.'

'Okay.' Maia nodded. She put her arm gently around the woman's shoulders and guided her back a few steps, turning her slightly so that Maia's own body partially shielded her view of the car. She manoeuvred her out of the way. Not far enough that she felt too removed but far enough that she wouldn't compromise the rescue and, more importantly, far enough away so she couldn't see too much. Maia expected the consequences to be traumatic and possibly tragic. This situation might not have a happy outcome and she didn't want the woman falling to pieces prematurely.

There was not even a whisper of sound from the car. It was ominously quiet. Maia and Henry exchanged a glance as Maia stepped away. The circumstances were far from good. The passenger side of the car was so badly damaged that it was almost unrecognisable and there was certainly no chance that Henry could access the car from that side. It was buried under rubble and the roof had caved in.

'What's your husband's name?' he asked the woman.

'Mark.'

Henry nodded and turned back to the car. He crawled inside through the driver's door. Dust still billowed in the air but Maia could just make out his figure through the haze. She could only assume that he was checking for a pulse.

There was a baby capsule strapped in to the back seat. Maia saw him reach towards the capsule but she knew he wouldn't be able to do anything from that position. The roof of the car was only inches from the top of the capsule, inches from the baby's head; he wouldn't have room to lift the baby out.

Henry backed out of the car. He didn't say anything. Maia assumed he didn't want the woman to panic, but he didn't shake his head either, and Maia knew that meant there was still hope. He jiggled the handle on the back door but the car was bent out of shape from the impact of the rubble and the door wouldn't budge.

He quickly marshalled bystanders; he couldn't afford to waste time. There were several burly young construction workers who must have been on a worksite nearby and were more than willing to lend a hand. They waited for Henry to explain what had happened before they began to lift wreckage off the car. Street signs, masonry, window frames and twisted metal were tossed aside.

Maia could feel the woman shaking. She needed to sit her down; she didn't think she could support her weight if she fainted or fell. The woman bent over, and Maia thought she was about to collapse, but then she straightened, clutching her daughter's dummy in her left hand.

'I think you should sit down,' Maia said. The

woman was trembling and Maia knew she was in shock. She guided her to a bench on the edge of the square, opposite her car. The woman didn't resist—in fact she was almost too compliant, something which worried Maia even more. She doubted she would be this calm faced with the same situation but Maia suspected it was the shock that was causing her composure. Shock could be fatal and Maia had no way of combating it if necessary. Not out here in these disastrous circumstances.

'My name is Maia,' she told her again. She knew Henry had already told her that but she doubted the woman remembered—she wouldn't expect her to—and Maia wanted to keep the woman focused on her. 'What's your name?'

'Susan,' the woman replied as she leant forward and put her elbows on her knees, resting her chin in her hands. She jiggled her knees up and down. Maia could tell she wanted to bury her face in her hands but was too afraid to take her eyes off the car. The car that trapped her family.

Susan stood up from the bench. She paced up and down liked a caged animal, worry and concern making her restless.

She stopped briefly and turned to Maia. 'Sienna is only thirteen months old. She has to be all right. This is all my fault.'

Maia stood up and put a hand on Susan's arm. 'This isn't your fault.'

'But it is,' Susan insisted. 'Sienna dropped her dummy. If I hadn't bothered to pick it up, we could have been on our way. We could have been gone from here, away from that building. Half a minute could have made all the difference.'

Maia didn't know what to say. She had no words of comfort. Despite the warmth of the summer's day, Susan was shivering, and Maia wished she had something to put around her, something that could trap some body heat, but she had nothing. Maia hadn't felt so useless since her father had passed away. She hated the sense of futility. She hated being unable to help. And then, in the midst of the car alarms, the yelling and the thump of bricks and concrete being tossed aside, they heard it.

A baby's cries.

Susan shot across the street, all traces of shakiness gone, as Maia followed in her wake.

Henry was back inside the car but there was no way he could lift Sienna out of the capsule from the front seat. There wasn't enough clearance. He'd have to remove the entire capsule but Maia didn't know how he would do that either. The capsule was firmly secured in the middle seat by the seatbelt and straps. Even if he could undo it he wouldn't be able to squeeze it between the two front seats.

Susan's arms were folded across her chest and she doubled over, as if in pain, as Sienna's cries continued.

Henry backed out of the car. 'Does anyone have a pocket knife of some description?' he asked the construction workers. 'I need to cut the straps on the baby seat.'

One of the guys, a solidly built Maori, stopped moving rubble and unclipped a pocket knife from his tool belt. He tossed it across the roof of the car to Henry, who caught it easily. He flicked it open before crawling back into the car and Maia could see him sawing at the straps that secured the capsule until finally it came free. Sienna had gone quiet. Maia knew Henry would be talking to her; perhaps she found his voice soothing or perhaps the rocking motion as he severed the straps had calmed her down. Once again, he backed out of the car, and Sienna's cries started again as he disappeared from her view. He straightened up and pulled his shirt out of his trousers. He undid a couple of buttons and pulled it over his head. The construction guys continued to remove the debris but Maia had forgotten all about them. Henry was standing in the middle of the street, half-naked, his torso completely bare. What the hell was he doing?

He held his shirt in one hand as he climbed back into the car. He draped his shirt over Sienna's capsule, tucking it underneath so she was completely enclosed, completely hidden, before backing out of the car again. His movements were quick but deliberate. Measured. He picked up a brick that was lying by his feet and Maia watched the muscles in his back and arm tense as he smacked it against the car window. The glass shattered, scattering little squares of safety glass through the car, and Maia finally understood why he'd removed his shirt. He'd needed something to protect Sienna.

He knocked the last remaining pieces of glass from the frame and reached through the window. He pulled the capsule across the back seat towards him. He carefully removed his shirt from over the top of Sienna and shook the glass off. He undid the buckles holding Sienna into her car seat and lifted her gently out of the car. She was still crying but it was a good sound. It was the sound of life.

'Sienna!' Susan reached for her baby. Her arms were outstretched as she stepped forward to take her from Henry, when the earth shuddered again. The movement wasn't as violent, nor was the tremor as powerful as the initial quake, but it was enough to trigger more panic and have everyone ducking for cover. Rescue attempts were abandoned as people bolted away from the buildings and into the street.

Henry dropped to the ground and Maia's heart dropped with him.

# CHAPTER SIX

HENRY CRADLED SIENNA to his chest as he knelt on the road, sheltering her as best as he could. Maia pulled Susan down to the ground too, glancing up to check Henry was all right. They were in open space but her survival instincts kicked in and made her want to make them as small a target as possible. Crouching on the ground probably wouldn't make any difference to their safety—surely the buildings around them couldn't collapse any further?—but it was her first response.

The tremor passed. This one had been of far shorter duration than the first, but the destruction wasn't over yet. Maia stood, aware that she was pulling Susan up with her, when she heard a second loud noise. She was on edge, which wasn't surprising, but it wasn't a very useful reaction. She recognised the sound now, it was becoming all too familiar: the sound of more buildings falling.

The destruction was overwhelming and Maia wasn't sure how much more she could take. She was desperate to get out of the city; self-preservation was a powerful motivator, but she wasn't prepared to leave Henry, and she knew Henry wouldn't be prepared to leave the city. He had unfinished business.

Once again everyone was stunned in the silence immediately following the tremor and it took several seconds for people to snap out of the disbelief and to remember what they were doing before the aftershock had rocked the street. Maia looked to Henry for guidance.

He was standing in the middle of the street, still holding baby Sienna. He looked calm and solid, a cool head in the face of the disaster. She had no idea how he managed it but his strength made her feel safe and secure.

Susan left Maia's side and went to Henry. He passed her baby over and Susan took her anxiously before retreating back to the bench in the square where she sat, cradling her child against her chest. Maia wasn't convinced that the bench was a safe place—she didn't know where safe was anymore—but at least there were no tall buildings on this edge of the square. The worst that could happen here was damage to the paving underfoot. Maia shook her head; no, the worst that could happen was that Susan could be widowed, but she didn't want to think about that. She was close to tears already and thinking about that would surely push her over the edge.

She turned her back on Susan and the cathedral. She couldn't stand to look at the damaged church with its caved-in walls and its massive spire lying in a pile of rubble. She really hoped that no one had been in the bell tower. It was a popular spot for tourists to get a good view over the city and she couldn't stand to think of how many people could be buried in there.

People were starting to panic now. Before the aftershock they'd been trying to help, battling to reach those trapped, fighting on, but now the flight response was kicking in. People everywhere were scrambling to safety but not Henry.

Maia couldn't let him do this on his own. If he was going to risk his life, she wasn't going to let him do it alone. She wanted to be by his side. She dodged the cracks and holes, the broken pipes and the mud and masonry that made the road a minefield, and went to Henry. She needed the reassurance and comfort that being with him would bring her.

The earth was quiet again. The terrible rumbling had ceased once more, leaving further chaos and carnage behind. Henry looked around at the deserted streets. People had fled in all directions but despite the mass exodus he wasn't alone. Maia was with him. And that was all he needed to know to keep going. He had saved the baby but there was more he needed to do.

He went around to the passenger side of the car where Mark was still trapped. If he was going to have any chance of saving this man, he needed to get him out of the vehicle. He wasn't certain that they would be able to get him out alive but he needed to try.

But the situation was grim. The left-hand side of the car was unrecognisable, buried under the fallen facade of the building. The roof was flattened by debris and only the back right-hand corner still looked anything like a car should. Henry couldn't be certain but it looked as if the wreckage that the construction workers had cleared before had been replaced by more debris following the aftershock.

He would need to start again.

He picked up the nearest brick and tossed it aside. Time was of the essence and this task was too big for one man. What he really needed was some extra muscle.

One of the construction crew, the big Maori who had lent Henry his knife, was still in the vicinity. He nodded at Henry and started once again to move rubble. He didn't waste energy on conversation; he just pitched in to help.

The pieces of fallen stone and concrete were large and it was heavy, back-breaking work. Within a few minutes Henry was puffing. He could feel his muscles straining and his skin was damp with sweat but the construction worker tossed the enormous blocks of masonry aside as if they were made of polystyrene, not concrete, and Henry vowed to keep going for as long as it took. He wouldn't give in, not while he had help. Not while there was a chance of saving Mark. He knew he would need to rely on the adrenalin that had kicked in and was coursing through his system but he refused to give up.

His hands were filthy, his knuckles were scraped and bleeding, and the muscles in his arms screamed with the effort, but he kept working. As he rolled another stone out of the way he saw Maia crawling into the car through the driver's door. He wanted to tell her not to, he wanted to tell her it wasn't safe, but he didn't. He knew she wouldn't listen to him and he wanted to know if Mark was still alive.

'Pulse is present but very weak.' Maia's voice floated out to him. 'I'm not sure if he's breathing. Mark? Can you hear me?' Maia tried to communicate with the man. 'There's been an earthquake. You're trapped in your car but we're working to get you out.'

Henry couldn't hear a response from Mark.

'He's unconscious.' Maia continued to update him. 'His head has fallen forward. It might be restricting his airway. His head is bleeding and his legs are trapped. I'm going to try to call an ambulance.'

There was a pause in Maia's commentary and, while he laboured, Henry imagined Maia contorting herself inside the car to reach her mobile phone and punch in the numbers.

'The network is busy!' She sounded agitated. 'How can the network be busy? 111 calls are given priority.'

Henry knew that in an emergency the phone network could block calls, only allowing calls to emergency numbers to get through. 'There must be an enormous volume of calls if you're getting a busy signal,' he replied, struggling for air as he tossed another lump of concrete aside.

Despite the gravity of the situation, he realised that not one ambulance had been past. Not that he'd noticed anyway. How many injured were there? What were the emergency crews facing? He wondered if the old lady with the broken hip had been collected. It was quite possible that she wasn't at the top of the list of casualties and was still lying on the ground. How many had already been injured or killed? How many more might die because of a lack of resources? What level of disaster was this?

Henry knew it was bad, but just exactly how bad they probably wouldn't know for a while.

If they got Mark out alive and there were no ambulances, what then? Was this a futile exercise?

Finally he cleared the last piece of masonry which allowed him enough space to get access to Mark from the passenger side. The passenger door had been ripped off—it must have been open when the quake hit—but at least that meant there was room for Mark to be extricated. That was fortunate as they would have had no hope of prising him out otherwise without assistance. They would have needed to wait for the fire brigade and the 'jaws of life'.

Henry could see Mark and Maia. She was still in the car. He wanted to get both of them out of there as quickly as possible. Mark needed urgent medical attention but Henry was also worried about more aftershocks. He didn't want to be on this street if there were more shocks coming and he definitely wanted Maia out of danger, out of harm's way. But Maia was still talking to Mark, who was still unresponsive.

Henry squatted down and reached into the car. His hands and nails were filthy—scratched, dirty and bleeding—but there was nothing he could do about that at present. He lifted Mark's eyelid with a dirty finger, first his left eyelid, then his right. It was difficult to see but he thought the right pupil contracted when exposed to light and wasn't so sure about the left. It was impossible to do a proper assessment, he didn't have the room or the equipment, but the situation was not looking good. Mark was barely breathing, he had a possible head injury, potential chest injuries and, from this side of the car, Henry could see that his left lower leg had been severely crushed by the compacted front of the car. He didn't like the look of that at all. In order for Mark to receive help they would need to negotiate getting him out of the car, but that looked almost impossible, given that the windscreen and dashboard had been compressed down hard onto his legs.

It was going to be a difficult and dangerous process to retrieve him and, depending on how badly damaged his left leg was, moving him could have dire consequences. Fatal, even.

Henry could only guess at the amount of blood Mark had lost. Blood loss, an almost certain drop in blood pressure, shock, a possible head injury; Mark's odds of survival were decreasing by the second, and if he did survive Henry suspected it might cost him his leg.

'What do we do now?' Maia asked.

They were both looking at the mess, assessing the situation and trying to work out a solution.

'I don't know. It's going to be difficult to get him out of here and I really don't want to move him until we have an ambulance on standby. He's critically injured.' Henry was at a loss but he refused to admit defeat. There had to be a way.

He looked around him but there were no answers, only chaos. A policeman was crossing the square. Finally, someone who might be able to help. Henry whistled loudly and waved his arms, attracting attention, and the copper came over to them.

'Are you able to get through to the emergency

services?' Henry asked. 'The network is blocked and this man needs to get to a hospital. He needs urgent medical attention and we need an ambulance.'

'There aren't any,' the policeman replied.

'What do you mean, there aren't any?'

'They're all busy. It's World War III around here. We've never needed so many ambulances all at once. There are more injured people than ambulances and the paramedics are working flat out.'

'This man is in a critical condition. Are you telling me there's nothing we can do?'

'I'm sorry, I know it's a tragedy, but I wouldn't count on getting an ambulance any time soon.'

'My ute is parked over there.' The construction worker interrupted Henry and the copper. 'It's no ambulance but do you reckon we could get him into the tray and I can take you to the hospital?'

It was a terrible option but it was also the only one on offer. Without urgent medical attention

Mark would die, and Henry knew Mark wasn't going to get that attention lying on the street. He might not make it, but he *definitely* wouldn't make it if they didn't try something. But it didn't mean that this was Henry's decision to make. He would need Maia's help if he was going to have any chance of pulling this off but he knew she might decide the risk was too great.

'Maia, will you help me?'

'You want to take him to hospital in the back of a ute?'

She obviously thought he was crazy.

'With his wife's permission,' Henry said, as if that was all he needed for this to work. 'I have to do something. If I do nothing, he'll die on the street.'

Maia looked at Mark and then back at Henry. He could see the concern in her eyes but then she nodded. She would help.

Henry didn't waste any more time. He turned back to the construction worker. 'I'm sorry, mate, I don't even know your name.'

'Dean.'

'I'm Henry.' They shook hands—an automatic and ridiculously civilised gesture in incredibly uncivilised surroundings—while Henry continued. 'Can you back your ute up as close as you can get while I talk to Mark's wife?'

Susan was huddled on the bench. She looked fragile. It would be a good idea for her to be checked out at the hospital too. Henry sat beside her. 'Mark is alive but he's critically injured. He needs to get to a hospital but there are no available ambulances. We can try to get him out of the car and then transport him in the back of that ute.' Henry pointed at Dean's vehicle as he was backing it up to Susan's car. 'It's not ideal but I believe it's his only chance. But it needs to be your decision.' He wasn't positive that Susan was in any state to be making this call but her answer, when it came, surprised him. She sounded strong and decisive.

'I can't let him die here. We have to try.'

Henry nodded and returned to the car. Dean

had manoeuvred his ute so that it sat at right angles to the rear of Susan's car. It was going to be an awkward retrieval. First they had to get Mark out of the car and then they would have to lift and carry him over the rubble. Henry hated to think of all the things that could go wrong. Were they going to do more harm than good?

But he didn't have a choice. If they did nothing, Mark had no chance.

'Okay. Let's do this.'

Dean had cleared some room in the back of his utility truck. Tool boxes, bags of cement and a ladder had been pushed to one side and amongst the tools Henry spied a length of rope and a tarpaulin.

'Dean, grab that tarp and that rope, we can use that,' he said as he started to plan the logistics of extricating Mark. 'Maia, I'll need you out here to help me.'

They really needed a cervical collar and a stretcher. A spinal board would be even better. A defibrillator and an airway might be handy.

Pain relief. Fluids. The list went on and on, but they had none of those things, and they didn't have time to waste. They had neither the time nor the equipment to remove him with the utmost care. They would have to do the best they could.

'I need to fashion a tourniquet for his leg before we attempt to move him.' Henry was holding the length of rope in his hands. He was going to use that as his tourniquet. He slid the rope under Mark's thigh and ran it around twice, pulling it firm before knotting it as tightly as he could. The next problem was getting Mark out of the car. His legs were still trapped under the dashboard.

'Have you got a crowbar in your truck—anything that we might be able to use to remove this dashboard?' Henry asked Dean. This was when the jaws of life would have been really useful. 'We won't get him out like this.'

'I've got this,' Dean replied.

The car's windscreen was a spiderweb of

lines. Smashed and damaged, it had shattered and was barely hanging on. Dean reached into the car and with one well-timed punch the entire windscreen fell out onto the bonnet. He moved around to the front of the car, reached over the bonnet and into the car through the hole where the windscreen had been moments before, grabbed the plastic dashboard and ripped it out with his bare hands.

'That worked.' Henry nodded in appreciation. 'Okay, next step. Maia, if you can support Mark's head and neck, I'll lift his body.' Henry worked through his plan aloud; it helped him to clarify the steps in his mind and meant that the others were on board with his plan as well. 'Dean, can you clear a bit of space behind us? We need a flat area to lay your tarp out; we'll use that as a makeshift stretcher to lift Mark into the ute.'

Henry left Dean to get on with that task while he had another look at the logistics of moving Mark. He saw his shirt wedged between the two front seats where he'd dropped it after lifting Sienna to safety. He pulled it free and wrapped it around Mark's legs, tying it tightly by the sleeves. Perhaps if he could support Mark's left leg by using his right, then all the pieces of Mark would come out of the car together.

'Ready?' He looked at Maia. Her face was streaked with dirt and her dark hair had come loose and curled around her face. The dark strands were coated with a layer of dust and she had flecks of paint stuck in her hair like confetti. Her brown eyes were huge in her face. She looked scared but she nodded. He was scared too. This was an awful situation.

Behind them Dean had prepared the tarpaulin. It was time.

Maia tucked herself in close to the car and reached carefully behind Mark, sliding her hands behind his head to cradle his head and neck. Henry stepped in beside her. His hips were touching hers as he slid one hand just above Mark's hips and his other hand above his knees.

He was worried about spinal injuries but the real danger was with Mark's neck. As long as Maia held firm they would be doing their best to minimise the risk.

'On three?' he said.

Maia nodded.

Henry closed his eyes and said a brief, silent prayer, hoping they would get Mark out in one smooth, or smooth-ish, movement. He tightened his grip and counted. 'One, two, three…'

Somehow they managed to free Mark and lay him on the tarpaulin without mishap. It was probably a good thing he was unconscious. His pulse was weak, he was barely breathing and his chest was rising unevenly, but he was alive. Now they had to get him into their makeshift ambulance.

'Dean? Are you okay to give us a hand with this next move?' Henry asked. Dean looked big and tough; Henry just hoped he could stomach the rather confronting sight of Mark's traumatised leg.

'No worries.' He sounded confident.

'Great. We'll take one side each. Maia, you look after Mark's head. Dean, roll up your side of the tarpaulin, get it as close to Mark as possible; that'll keep him stable.' Henry watched, making sure Dean followed his instructions to the letter. 'We'll put him into the ute feet first.'

Dean had dropped the sides of his utility down so they had easier access and with Mark cocooned in the tarp this part of the transfer was much easier. Henry and Dean slid Mark's unconscious form onto the tray while Maia kept his head as still as she was able. Once Mark was safely ensconced, Maia and Henry climbed in with him. They would have to act as the medical team en route to the hospital. Not that there was much they could do except try to stop him from being buffeted around too much.

Susan hovered by the vehicle. She kissed Mark's forehead before climbing into the cab, still clutching baby Sienna. Dean lifted the panels on the side of the tray, sliding the catches into place as Henry urged Maia to swap places with him. She looked wiped out. She'd done enough; he would take responsibility for Mark.

'We need to get him to the Queen Liz,' Henry told Dean. 'Do you know the way?'

Dean nodded.

'Take it carefully, not too slow, but avoid as many potholes and bumps as you can,' Henry instructed.

'No worries,' Dean said as he climbed into the front seat.

Henry sat with his legs either side of Mark's head and shoulders as he stabilised his neck. The metal tray of the ute was uncomfortable but he barely noticed. It was going to be a long, slow, bumpy ride to the hospital but what other choice did they have? They had none.

Maia sat on a bag of cement beside Mark's inert form. She had her knees bent, her feet tucked against her bottom. She looked exhausted but she had coped brilliantly. He couldn't have managed without her. 'Are you okay?' he asked her.

She nodded. 'I think so.'

They were both filthy, covered in plaster dust and dirt, streaked white and brown. He licked his lips as he watched the world go by. His throat and lips were dry and his tongue felt swollen and was caked in dust. He could taste it. He would kill for a drink of water.

He was only vaguely aware that he was half-dressed, sitting bare-chested in the back of a ute as it crawled out of the CBD. His shirt was wrapped around Mark's legs, it was torn and bloodied and would never be worn again, and his cotton trousers were damp and splattered with mud. He could see some dark, dried blood on Maia's forearm and shirt. Neither of them had gloves or any sort of protection. His hands were filthy and he was worried about infection but again, with limited options, there was noth-ing more he could do until they reached the hospital—there was every chance that Mark wouldn't survive the journey anyway.

Traffic was moving slowly but the roads were dangerous. The bitumen was riddled with wide cracks and deep holes, and the traffic lights were all out, adding to the chaos. Dean had to negotiate the damaged roads as well as piles of fallen masonry, and dazed and confused pedestrians. Everyone was desperately trying to get out of the city. People were driving on the wrong side of the road, which increased the level of confusion, and pedestrians wandered like zombies onto the street without looking. It was like the apocalypse.

Red and blue lights flashed through the dusty haze. The fire department had joined the rescue effort. They had their ladders extended up building fronts and were rescuing people from windows and roofs of collapsed buildings, but their efforts were being hampered as several buildings had caught fire, adding to the danger. The burst water mains meant there was no water connected to the fire hydrants so the fires burnt uncontrollably.

Dean's ute bumped over the cracks in the mud-covered road and Henry could smell sewage and gas. Their vehicle joined a convoy of civilian cars heading out of the city as army trucks and the fire department's urban search-and-rescue vehicles took their place. Half a dozen water tankers followed the army trucks and Henry realised these were for the fire brigade. It was the only way they had to try to fight and contain the fires.

Helicopters, both army and media, buzzed overhead, and the sirens of the emergency vehicles could be heard near and far, but there was surprisingly little human noise. People were being assisted, and in some instances carried, from the rubble but along the side of the road Henry could see the shapes of those who had not been so lucky, their bodies covered with makeshift shrouds.

There were coordinated calls from search and

rescuers—official and unofficial—but no distressed screams, no loud crying. Henry wondered whether people were afraid to add to the stress and tension, or perhaps they didn't have the energy to spare on superfluous noise or were too shocked. Even he and Maia were silent. But there was nothing for them to say. There was nothing more they could do.

He looked back at Maia. She hadn't moved. Her chin was resting on her knees as she stared into the distance and clutched the tarpaulin, trying to minimise the rolling motion. She looked sad and Henry longed to comfort her.

She was smeared with dirt and blood but she still looked beautiful. Heartbreakingly sad and beautiful. Her hair was a wild mess. Dark tendrils framed her face and fell over one eye and he wanted so badly to reach out and brush her hair back from her face. He knew exactly how traumatic these events would have been for her. He'd been through something similar before and he knew nothing could prepare you for the first time you experienced a disaster on this scale.

The breeze created by the movement of the vehicle carried a scent to him, the scent of frangipanis, sunshine and summer. Maia's scent. He'd missed her smell.

Was it really possible that he could smell her? It was ridiculous to think that he could smell something so sweet over and above the stench of the streets but he breathed deeply regardless, taking in his fill of Maia.

The idea was a pleasant distraction as they drove back to the Queen Liz. Back to where they had started their day. It was incredible to think it was only a few hours ago that they had been sitting in the darkened lecture theatre. Incredible to think about what had happened in those intervening hours. Thousands of lives had changed in that time, some lives had ended. It just demonstrated to him how important it was to make every minute count. Nothing could be wasted or taken for granted.

Maia had taken her mobile phone out of her pocket. She was typing a message with her thumb as she kept hold of the tarpaulin with her other hand. He wondered who she was texting. Her mother? Todd?

Maia paused and looked up at him, her dark eyes shining with unshed tears. 'How bad do you think this is?' she asked.

'I don't know.' He was supposed to be the expert but he had no way of knowing the extent of the damage that the quake had caused. He suspected that the CBD had been hardest hit but that was only a guess. His gut was telling him it was bad but he wasn't going to share that feeling with Maia. He wasn't prepared to make a bad situation worse.

'I'm worried about Mum and my sisters. The phone network is busy but do you think a text will get through?'

That was something he did know. 'There's more chance that a text will go through—maybe not straight away, but it will send at some point.'

He thought it would likely be some time before the phone network was free again but he knew how important it was for Maia to feel like she was doing something. He knew exactly how overwhelming and distressing the feeling of hopelessness and helplessness could be in these situations.

He could see her hand trembling as she pressed the keys on her phone. He was worried about her. She was shaking quite noticeably and he suspected she was in shock. That wasn't surprising, the events of the day had been extremely traumatic and the day wasn't over yet. He wanted desperately to take her in his arms and comfort her. To tell her everything would be okay. To tell her she'd been magnificent today. To tell her everything would be all right. But he couldn't do that. He didn't have the answers and, even if he had, Maia wasn't his to comfort. Not anymore.

The knowledge that Maia was marrying some-one else was cutting him to the core. He hadn't been able to commit to her and she'd moved on without him. She was marrying someone else and there wasn't anything he could do about it. He wasn't the type to destroy someone else's relationship. If she was happy, then he'd be happy for her. He'd learn to be happy and, if he couldn't learn, he'd pretend.

He longed to comfort her but he had lost that privilege. Maia had moved on and he would have to accept that Todd had Maia's heart. For now, and perhaps for always.

# CHAPTER SEVEN

DEAN PULLED HIS vehicle into the emergency entrance of the Queen Liz and came to a stop behind a row of ambulances. The ambulance bay was a hive of activity; medics were thick on the ground and Henry assumed they'd been going nonstop for some time.

'We need some help here,' he called out loudly, drawing attention to their arrival. He didn't want to be overlooked in the chaos, mayhem and madness. He couldn't afford any more delays. Not if they wanted to give Mark a chance.

Maia moved around to the rear of the tray and her hands replaced Henry's as she continued to stabilise Mark's neck. Their movements were coordinated and fluid as a silent understanding of what needed to be done passed between them. Henry leapt out of the ute and began to drop the sides as a trauma team joined them.

'Male in his thirties. Unconscious but breathing,' he said, giving them a summary of Mark's condition. 'Crush injuries, possible head injury, severe blood loss, major trauma to his left lower leg. We pulled him from a car but were only able to give very basic first aid at the scene.' He and Maia stepped back as the trauma team took over. Their involvement ended here but it was difficult to just walk away. They waited and watched while Mark was lifted onto a stretcher and rushed inside. Susan trailed in the wake of the medics, holding baby Sienna close. Blood continued to run from her head wound but Henry knew she wouldn't seek treatment until she knew that Mark was being taken care of.

Mark's stretcher disappeared through the emergency doors and two paramedics emerged in his place. One of them was Todd.

He didn't notice Henry, or if he did he didn't acknowledge him. His eyes went straight to Maia.

He was by her side in three strides. 'Maia!' He wrapped his arms around her and Maia burst into tears. 'Are you all right? What happened to you?'

Henry could see Maia shaking but it was impossible to tell if it was from shock or her tears. Despite the heat of the day he could see goose bumps on her arms and her tears made her incapable of speech.

Todd looked over her head at Henry as Maia cried against his shoulder. 'What happened?' he asked him. 'Is she hurt?'

'No.' Henry shook his head. 'She's fine. Just in shock. We were in the city on our way back to the Children's and got caught up in the middle of the quake. We're only here because we brought a casualty in to the hospital.'

Todd nodded, put his hands on Maia's shoulders and gently stood her back. 'Maia, sweetheart, are you really okay?' He brushed her hair from her eyes and wiped a tear from her face. Henry felt a pang of longing. He wanted to be allowed to do that. He wanted to be the one who had permission to comfort her.

Maia sniffed and nodded.

Todd pressed his lips into the side of Maia's head as he cradled her face in his hands. 'I'm sorry,' he said, 'But I have to go. I have to get back into the city.'

Henry felt like a voyeur, witnessing this exchange, and he wondered if he should give them some privacy. But before he could drag himself away Todd turned to him again. 'Will you take care of her?' he asked.

'Of course,' Henry replied automatically.

Todd kissed Maia softly on her forehead. 'I'll see you later,' he said as he left her in Henry's care and returned to his ambulance.

'Do you need a ride somewhere or are you staying here?'

Henry glanced to his right. Dean was standing beside him. Maia still hadn't spoken and Henry was worried about her. She needed something to eat and a place to sit down and regroup. Todd had left Maia in his care, he'd given him permission to take care of her, but what Henry wanted was permission to comfort her, which was something entirely different.

Henry was conflicted. He thought he should probably take Maia inside to the hospital to get her checked out but he had a better idea. He knew she was only in mild shock. He'd keep an eye on her. She would be fine. He'd make sure of it.

'We're not staying here,' he told Dean. 'We need to get to the Children's Hospital.' He'd promised to take care of her and he'd be able to do that at the Children's. Maia should probably go home but Henry would be needed at the Children's and he wasn't about to send Maia off on her own. He didn't know how to get her home in any case and until he knew what the state of play was there for her he wasn't potentially going to put her into a traumatic situation. She'd heard nothing back from her mother as yet and he hoped that wasn't ominous. 'Could you give us a lift?'

'Course. No worries.'

Maia was wedged into the front seat of the ute, between Dean and Henry. She couldn't believe they'd managed to get Mark to hospital without killing him. When Henry had asked if she'd help she hadn't really considered the consequences. He'd needed her help and she'd offered it without a second thought. She trusted him, and if he'd thought it was a risk worth taking she wouldn't second guess him, but she couldn't believe it had turned out okay. So far. Who knew what would happen now for Mark? But at least they'd got him to the hospital alive. They'd done their best.

Dean had the windows up and the airconditioning on and Maia was feeling claustrophobic and cold. She was still shaking. She trembled against Henry's shoulder. She crossed her arms over her chest but she couldn't seem to stop the quivering.

Henry reached for the climate control and switched the airconditioning off. 'Do you mind if we have this off and put the windows down instead?' he asked Dean.

He wrapped his arm around her back and Maia tensed as his hand brushed the nape of her neck. If she'd been able to speak she would have asked him what he was doing but she was shaking so hard her teeth were chattering and talking was almost impossible. He rubbed her arms, attempting to warm her up, and her body responded to his touch, coming to life under his fingers. She could feel the blood begin to flow through her veins but his touch did more than warm her skin. His touch lit a fire inside her that spread from her belly to her limbs.

She was pressed against his chest. His naked, shirtless chest. He was still half-dressed. His shirt had disappeared into the Queen Liz, wrapped around Mark's legs.

Henry had a nasty gash on his left pectoral muscle and several grazes on his abdominals. Maia tried to ignore them. She tried to pretend he wasn't half-naked and she wasn't pressed against him. No one at the Queen Liz had batted an eyelid at his semi-naked state—it wasn't the most unusual thing they had seen today or any day—and Maia had also forgotten that he was only semi-clothed. Until now.

She closed her eyes, trying to ignore his proximity. She couldn't move away. There was nowhere to go and she knew she didn't really want to. It was comforting to be held in Henry's arms. But, while closing her eyes meant she couldn't see his sculpted chest or the ridge of his abdominals or the light dusting of hair that covered his pectoral muscles, her other senses took over. Now she could smell him.

All three of them were coated with dirt and a trace of dust lingered in the air but Maia could smell something extra on Henry. He'd worked up a sweat trying to free Mark from the car and the sweat had dried, leaving something warm and a little bit salty overlaying his familiar citrus scent but there was something more: the metallic scent of iron. The distinctive smell of blood. His own or Mark's—she didn't know. It could be his. She would need to clean and dress those cuts and scrapes on his torso when they got to the Children's Hospital.

She finally stopped shaking. Henry's body heat and the touch of his hands had warmed her to the point where she could sit still. She thought she might even be able to talk again.

Her phone beeped with an incoming message. She fished it out of her pocket, trying not to move out of Henry's embrace as she swiped the screen. It was a text from her mother.

'Is everything okay?' Henry asked.

Maia nodded. 'It's Mum. She's fine and so are the girls, the house too. We have no power and no water but we do still have a house. She'll send updates on the extended family as she hears more.'

'Good news, then.'

It was very good news and Maia's heart lifted as Dean dropped them off in front of the Children's Hospital. She felt she could cope with anything else the day wanted to throw at her now that she knew her family and Todd were okay.

The contrast between here and the Queen Liz was remarkable. There was none of the chaos, no sense of drama and urgency, no evidence of trauma teams, no frantic arrival and departure of ambulances. One ambulance was just leaving and that was the extent of the activity.

They walked side by side into the emergency department. The waiting area was empty. Eerily quiet. Carrie was the only person there. She raced over to them as if expecting them to collapse at any moment. Maia wasn't surprised. She knew they looked like walking wounded. They were filthy, bloody and dishevelled.

'Oh, my God, are you two all right?'

'We're fine,' Henry said as he headed straight

for the water cooler. He poured two cups of cold water and handed one to Maia before draining his own in a single gulp.

Water had never tasted as sweet nor as good, Maia thought as she washed away the layer of dust that coated her tongue and throat. They re-filled their cups several times as Carrie paced impatiently, waiting for answers.

'You're not hurt?' Carrie looked them up and down, inspecting them for injuries. 'You've both got blood all over you, and Henry, you're cov-ered in cuts.'

'They're not serious,' Henry said, shrugging off her concern. 'And most of the blood isn't ours. We were coming back through the city when the quake hit. We stopped to help.'

'According to the reports we've had the CBD has been hit hard,' Carrie said.

Henry nodded. 'It's a disaster. It looks like the images you see on the news of cities after a bomb blast. Was that where the worst dam-age was?'

Carrie nodded and confirmed Henry's earlier suspicions.

'It was the most horrific thing I've ever experienced,' Maia added. Despite the rather regular frequency of earthquakes in Christchurch this one really had been the most frightening one Maia had ever felt. The force of the quake and the scale of the disaster were like nothing they had ever experienced before. 'Buildings were collapsing like decks of cards; they fell on people and cars and buses. There were fires and floods and bodies everywhere. It was horrible. The bell tower of the cathedral is gone—we were almost under it when it fell—and the Press Building has been destroyed. It was terrifying.' Now that she was out of danger she could admit how frightened she'd been.

'Brenda's husband works in the Press Building,' Carrie said.

'Keith?' In the stress of the day Maia had forgotten that she knew someone in that building.

Carrie was nodding. 'Brenda hasn't heard

from him.' Her voice caught in her throat and Maia could see the question in her eyes. 'No news is good news, right?'

Maia wasn't so sure. She remembered the noise as the roof had caved in and the sight of tonnes of building material crashing into the office space below. She'd seen the devastation in the city and watched that building and others collapse. She'd seen the bodies of the victims lying on the street and she knew there would be more to come. But there was nothing she could do and what could she say?

She turned to Henry. She could feel herself starting to shake once more. 'What do we tell Brenda?'

'Nothing,' he replied. 'We don't have any details. Any facts. Hopefully she might not think to ask us. Anything we say would be supposition—that's not helpful. If she can't contact her husband, the police or Urban Search and Rescue are the ones who will give her any news, and only when they know for certain. She doesn't need to know we've been in the city.' He looked from Maia to Carrie. He knew what it was like to be given false hope and he didn't want to put someone else in that situation. He waited for their nod of agreement before he continued. 'We came back here to lend a hand but I didn't expect it to be so quiet.'

'We had a few patients brought in early,' Carrie said. 'But, touch wood, there doesn't appear to have been too many children hurt.'

Maia rapped her knuckles against her head in a superstitious gesture as Carrie continued. 'The epicentre of the quake was at Lyttelton, and the worst of the damage is on that side of the city through to the CBD, but we're expecting the overflow of adult patients from the other hospitals. There are already hundreds injured and of course that toll is expected to climb. I think we're about to be run off our feet. We're about to test your new system.'

'We need to get cleaned up, then,' Henry said, in control and in charge.

'We're running on generators and we've got no water for showers. The best you'll be able to do is the antibacterial hand sanitisers and then antiseptic wipes,' Carrie told him. 'Do you need me to get you anything?'

'I don't think so. Thanks,' Maia said as she and Henry headed for a treatment cubicle.

'Okay, I'll let Brenda know you're here and leave you to it,' Carrie said as she bounced off.

They were both filthy—dusty, blood-stained and sweaty. Hand sanitisers and wipes were not going to cut it. Maia took two empty bowls from a cupboard and told Henry to follow her. She filled the bowls from the water cooler and gave them to Henry to take back to the cubicle while she fetched two sets of surgical scrubs. She ducked into the change room and quickly stripped off her own filthy clothes before grabbing some hand towels from the linen supply.

She returned to the cubicle and dropped the clean scrubs beside the sink before soaking a towel in the bowl of cool water and handing it to Henry. 'The water might be a bit fresh but we'll have to wipe some of the dirt off before we can hope to get decently clean.' She soaked a second towel for herself and wiped her face and arms, removing as much of the dirt and dust as she could, while Henry did the same. She threw the towel in the dirty linen bag and took her engagement ring off to put it onto her necklace so she could clean her hands properly.

As she removed it she noticed that one of the claws holding the diamond into the setting had been bent. She must have caught it on something while they'd been evacuating Mark. She checked to make sure the stone wasn't loose and wasn't in danger of falling out before she slid the ring onto the chain and fastened it around her neck. She felt terrible that she'd damaged the ring; thank God she hadn't lost the stone.

She plunged her hands into the bowl of cool water and scrubbed her nails. Henry was still wiping over his chest and arms but she tried to keep her eyes averted. She didn't need that distraction. She was managing quite well until she heard him inhale quickly, as if he was in pain. She looked up and could see that the cut on his left pectoral muscle had started to bleed as he'd wiped the towel across his chest.

'Sit down and I'll do your back for you,' she told him. 'And then I'll attend to those cuts.' She had offered to help clean him up. She gave him a clean towel. 'Put some pressure on that cut,' she said as she took a second fresh towel, soaked it and wiped it over Henry's back. She ran the cloth over his shoulders slowly, enjoying the feel of his warm skin under her fingers. It was an intimate motion.

She finished his back and moved around to stand in front of him. He had always been muscular but lean—he'd played on the wing in the university rugby team—but he'd bulked up over the past three years and still looked good. Really good. His shoulders were square and broad, the muscles in his arms well-defined, his chest hair dark, his stomach flat and his abdominals ripped.

She wiped a few traces of dirt from his chest, avoiding the more serious cuts. She pulled on a pair of gloves and concentrated hard on cleaning his injuries, putting antiseptic and dressings on. There was a nasty gash on the inside of his right arm, another one on his left chest and several grazes over his abdominals from leaning into the car. Maia could feel his body heat radiating from him and her hands shook as she applied antiseptic ointment to the cut on his chest.

'Are you okay?' he asked.

'I'm fine.' It wasn't fatigue or even shock that was making her jittery now, it was her proximity to a semi-naked Henry that was making her wobble, but she wasn't going to admit defeat. She didn't want someone else to take over; she didn't want anyone else getting this close to him. She was perfectly capable of finishing what she'd started.

But, standing this close, she wasn't really sure

where to look, what was appropriate. She focused on the dimple in his chin. She'd always loved that. Along with his full lips the dimple added a bit of softness to his very masculine features. His strong brow, chiselled cheekbones and square jaw were all softened by the dimple. She was tempted to run her thumb over it but instead she opened another dressing pack and carefully placed it over the cut on his chest.

All that was left now was the cut on the inside of his right biceps. She took his elbow in her hand and turned his arm out, exposing the paler flesh of his upper arm.

'Are you up to date with your tetanus shots?' she asked as she put the last dressing on and gathered up the rubbish.

'Yes.'

Maia turned to the bin to throw the rubbish away. 'You need to get…' She turned back as she spoke and was confronted by the sight of Henry bending over to pull his trousers off over his feet. He was wearing navy boxer shorts, she couldn't help but notice, and very little else. His bottom was round and firm and perfect.

He straightened up, holding his trousers in one hand.

He stood in front of her, now almost totally naked. His boxer shorts had a white band of elastic at the waist. It made his olive skin look darker than it would normally and drew her eye.

No, that wasn't what was drawing her eye. His shorts were a snug fit and left very little to the imagination. Not that she needed to rely on her imagination—she'd seen it all before. Many times. But she shouldn't be looking there now.

'I need to get what?' Henry said, reminding her that she had been halfway through a sentence, but Maia had completely lost her train of thought. She'd been completely and utterly distracted by the sight of a nearly naked Henry and her brain was having difficulty thinking about anything except Henry in boxer shorts.

She blushed and swallowed hard as she lifted

her eyes to his face and tried to remember what she'd been going to say. 'Dressed,' she said.

He grinned; his perfect, full lips parted, showing off his even white teeth as he laughed. 'That wasn't what you were going to say.'

He was right, it wasn't. It wasn't even what she really wanted. But she shouldn't be so happy to stand here and ogle a semi-naked man, be it Henry or otherwise. 'No, I was going to suggest that you get some antibiotics,' she said when she remembered what the end of her sentence should have been.

'Sorry,' he apologised. 'I didn't mean to make you uncomfortable. I needed to change my clothes and I didn't stop to think.' He didn't look sorry. He was smiling, the dimple in the centre of his chin had disappeared and his eyes sparkled with amusement.

'It's okay.' She was a nurse after all. She'd seen plenty of naked bodies, although not many had been quite so spectacular.

Henry cleared his throat, and she realised

her eyes had drifted south again, but there was nothing she could do. She was transfixed, mesmerised, hypnotised by the sight of him. His hips were lean, his thighs were strong and powerful, and Maia could feel her heart pounding.

She forced her eyes back to his face.

His eyes had turned dark with desire. She could see it in his expression. His indigo-blue eyes were devouring her, poring over her as if she too were naked.

He was standing mere inches from her. She had nowhere to go, nowhere to hide. She was trapped between the bench and a smiling and almost completely naked Henry.

# CHAPTER EIGHT

HENRY REACHED PAST her and it took all her self-control and willpower not to step in towards him, not to close those last few centimetres and press herself up against his naked flesh. His arm brushed against hers as he reached for the clean set of scrubs that she'd left on the bench. This time he was touching her. It felt different from when she'd been touching him, from when she'd been running the cloth over his bare skin. Now he was in control. Before, she had held the upper hand.

She could feel his breath on her cheek as he leant towards the counter. She pressed herself backwards, and felt the hard edge of the bench top digging into her lower back, but the discomfort wasn't enough to distract from her reaction to Henry's proximity. Her nipples peaked in response to his breath on her cheek, to the touch of his arm. A ripple of desire shot through her, running from her breasts to the junction of her thighs, turning her legs to jelly. She pressed herself harder against the bench, knowing that was the only thing holding her up. Why was her body intent on betraying her? Betraying Todd? Because that was what it felt like. She'd made a promise to Todd but her body was making it difficult to keep.

What was she doing? She was engaged to be married. She needed to remember herself and her promises. Her father would be shocked and horrified if he could see her now. He valued loyalty and family above anything else. He had considered Todd family and there was no greater sin than to be disloyal to your family. She picked up the scrubs and handed them to Henry, forcing him to move back as she stepped around him. 'You're all done.' Her voice wobbled as she tried to get herself under control. 'I'll see you outside,' she added before she fled from the cubicle.

By six in the evening Maia was physically and emotionally exhausted. She'd been working nonstop treating myriad patients, mostly adults who were being diverted from the Queen Liz and who were presenting with simple fractures, concussions, burns, chest pain and respiratory complaints. She wasn't having to deal with anything that was overly taxing medically but the emotional trauma for a lot of these patients was sometimes more harrowing than their physical injuries.

Hospitals around the city couldn't cope with the influx of injured, and people with minor injuries—cuts, abrasions and minor burns—were being turned away and sent instead to doctor's surgeries and first-aid facilities that had been set up in the suburbs. The injury toll was already into the thousands and continuing to climb.

Patients with more serious fractures or multiple fractures as well as internal injuries were being taken into surgery. The surgeons, including Henry, and theatre staff were being kept busy too.

Updates were coming through from the emergency services. The ambulance officers were the main source of information but there was also a battery-powered radio on the desk and, although the volume was kept low, it was enough to enable them to catch the occasional news broadcast.

The television screen in the emergency department which usually showed children's programmes was blank. No power in the city meant no television, which meant no live crosses to the disaster zones, which Maia thought was a good thing. No one needed to watch images of the disaster. They were living it.

Fifty-eight had been confirmed dead but still that toll was expected to rise. There would be no quick fix to the situation. The search and rescue and recovery would go on throughout the night.

Time was critical. Fortunately it was summer so the temperature and exposure to the elements weren't significant risk factors but the serious injuries people were anticipated to have sustained meant that the longer they went untreated or unrecovered increased the chance that they wouldn't make it. Death from trauma, asphyxia, burns and acute respiratory distress due to the dust in the air were all very real possibilities and infection would get more people.

But there wasn't time to think about what would happen in the next week or even tomorrow. Patients continued to arrive and as Maia finished with another case she got news that another ambulance was on its way. She headed for the loading bay.

'Maia, what are you still doing here?' Henry had been in Theatre for the past few hours but he appeared to be between cases now. 'You look exhausted. Why haven't you gone home?'

She felt dreadful but she didn't need to be told she looked it too. 'I can't get home. The buses aren't running and I don't have a car,' she told him.

'At least take a break, then. I'll figure something out but you need to sit down before you fall down.'

She wobbled on her feet as fatigue swamped her.

Henry caught her. He held her by her elbow and she leaned against him with relief. It felt good to have someone there to take care of her. It felt good that it was Henry.

'Have you had anything to eat?' he asked.

She frowned. They'd missed lunch. 'Breakfast?' That was hours ago, before the morning's seminar. Was it still the same day? It felt like she'd lived a whole week.

'The kitchen has just delivered some platters of sandwiches to the staff room. Will you please go and eat something? I promised Todd I'd look after you,' he said, reminding her that she wasn't really his responsibility and he wasn't hers to lean on.

'I'll just get this patient inside and then I'll have something to eat,' she said as the ambulance pulled in.

She saw Henry open his mouth, and knew he was about to argue his point with her, but before he could say anything the rear doors of the ambulance opened and Todd climbed out.

He looked like he'd been in the trenches. It was the only time Maia could remember that he didn't look immaculate. The knees of his uniform were caked in mud and his top was splattered with dirt and blood. But his first concern was for her. 'Maia, are you all right?'

Was he about to tell her how dreadful she looked too?

'She's exhausted. She needs to go home.' Henry answered for her before she'd had a chance to speak.

Great, now she would have two of them trying to tell her what was best for her. She opened her mouth to protest against being spoken about as though she was a child but she was too tired to argue. Add in some drama, fatigue and light-headedness from hunger, and she was really struggling. But she wasn't prepared to be sent on her way just yet. 'Don't worry about me,' she said. 'What have you got?'

Todd pulled a stretcher from the ambulance. A boy of about ten lay there, his face as white as the sheet that covered him. 'This is Patrick. Aged eleven. Crush injuries chest and torso, fractured arm, clavicle and probably scapula. BP one hundred over sixty. Pulse one-twenty. He was having a dentist appointment in the city and the building collapsed. He's had IV morphine, respiration monitored, rate fifteen.'

Poor kid, Maia thought; if he didn't like the dentist before he was going to hate it now.

Todd's paramedic partner, Jeremy, and Patrick's mum climbed out of the front of the ambulance.

'X-rays first,' Henry said as they wheeled Patrick into the hospital, where they were met by Brenda.

'I'll take over for you, Maia,' Brenda told her. 'You need to take a break, have something to eat. Have you boys eaten?' she asked Todd and Jeremy. 'There are sandwiches in the staff room,' she said. 'You can help yourselves once we've got this young man sorted.'

Maia didn't bother arguing. She went into the staff kitchen and looked longingly at a chair but she was reluctant to sit down. She was pretty sure that once she sat she wouldn't be able to make herself get up again.

Todd and Jeremy joined her but they didn't hesitate, sitting down and tucking straight into the food.

Maia gave in. She took an egg-and-salad sandwich and a beef-and-mustard one and sat while Todd got up and made coffee. She had just finished her second half sandwich and was debating about a third when Brenda came in.

'Thanks for your help today, Maia. I think we'll manage from here on. Why don't you go home?'

'Did Henry tell you to send me home?' Maia could tell Henry had been in her ear.

'Maia, you're not even supposed to be at work today,' Brenda went on. 'I appreciate your help, we all do, but I need you to get some rest. I need you back on deck tomorrow and I can't afford to have my nurses exhausted. Tired nurses make mistakes.'

'And what about you? When are you going to have a rest?'

'When Keith is found.'

'Has there been any news?' Maia knew that Brenda had been going flat out, trying to keep herself too busy to think about her missing husband.

Brenda shook her head. 'No and that's why I'm staying. I want to be here in case Keith is brought in. I'll feel better if I stay close to the action. I've asked the ambos and the Queen Liz to let me know if he's taken somewhere else.'

That was fair enough. Maia knew she would feel the same.

Todd drained his cup of coffee. 'We'll drop you home on our way back to the station, Maia. Have you heard from your mum? Is everything okay at home?'

She knew what he was asking. Was there a house and family to go home to?

'It's all good,' she said as fatigue finally got the better of her. Suddenly going home seemed like a very good idea. She didn't argue any further. She fetched her filthy clothes from the change rooms, and once Todd and Jeremy were ready to go she went with them. She didn't see Henry on her way out; he was probably back in Theatre, maybe operating on Patrick. She wondered if and when he'd get to leave.

Jeremy took a seat in the rear of the ambulance and offered Maia the front seat with Todd. Maia moved a bright yellow hard hat and high-visibility jacket to the floor and climbed up. Todd reached over and put his hand on her thigh before he started the engine. 'Are you really okay?'

'Yes, I'm fine.' Todd's hand was warm, she

could feel it through the thin cotton of her scrubs, but his touch didn't make her heart race or her body feel as if it might self-combust. What was wrong with her? Was it just fatigue? Why didn't she respond to Todd in the same way her body responded to Henry? Was he too familiar? Was it the forbidden element with Henry?

She put her hand over the top of his as she tried to remember what she would do in these situations normally, even though nothing about today felt remotely normal. 'You're the one I'm worried about,' she said. 'You're the one who has to keep returning to the danger zone.' At least she could say the right things, even if she wasn't feeling them.

They turned left at the River Avon and skirted the city. The streets leading into the CBD had been blocked off with temporary barriers, set up in chicanes to allow only the emergency crews through. Todd could have driven the ambulance through the city but there was no need to. It would be quicker to circumnavigate it and he would be back to help soon enough.

'How are things looking in there?' Maia asked. She could see police cars, ambulances, fire engines and armoured troop carriers, as well as trucks transporting generators and floodlights. Being summer, the sun wouldn't set until late—it wouldn't get dark until around nine o'clock—but Maia knew the emergency crews would be working through the night.

'It's bad, Maia. Really bad. We've never seen anything like it. The quake was a magnitude of six-point-three, but it was only five kilometres below the surface and the damage is just incredible. You saw the buildings around the square. Multiply that tenfold. I don't think there's a building left standing in the CBD that isn't damaged, if it's been left standing at all.'

'Did you see the cathedral?' she asked. Even now, just thinking about the state of the glorious old building made her feel like crying. Their wedding was supposed to be held there in four weeks' time. That was one decision they'd made about the wedding that she hadn't minded. Although she would have been just as happy to get married in a park or on the beach, her dad had loved the cathedral and she'd felt that was a decision he would have approved of.

'I did.'

'I'm terrified to think how many people might have been in the bell tower when it collapsed.'

'The canine search-and-rescue team have been brought in. From what I've heard, the dogs haven't found any trace of people in there.'

Maia sighed with relief. Finally some good news. 'I don't think I could bear to get married in there if people have been killed.'

Todd looked at her very briefly. 'It's not a sign, Maia. It doesn't mean anything other than the building wasn't built to withstand a quake of this force. This was a natural disaster, nothing more. But I should tell you, I don't think we'll be getting married there regardless. There's no way that building will be declared safe.'

Of course it wouldn't. Maia had seen the devastation for herself but she hadn't stopped to think what it would mean for them. 'Oh.'

'Don't worry. I'll sort something out,' Todd was quick to reassure her. 'The only sign you need to worry about is the one that says we are all okay. You and me and your family.'

His comment made her think about all the other families that weren't so lucky. 'How are the people in Lyttelton?' she asked. The suburb at the centre of the quake was only ten kilometres from the city. She'd seen the extent of the destruction in town and wondered how much worse things were at the centre of it all.

'It's odd,' Todd replied. 'The worst of the damage is actually in the city. There haven't been any reported fatalities in Lyttelton itself, not so far anyway. I guess I'll find out more as the night unfolds.'

'You'll be working all night?' she asked. 'Won't someone relieve you?'

'I doubt it. There just aren't enough of us to

go around. We can't stop until everyone is accounted for and it will take time for other crews to arrive from around the country to assist us. The airport is still closed. There are teams arriving by road from the rest of the country but they have to fly into the south island and then drive here. The Australians are coming too but until others arrive we'll have to manage. Even with help we'll be working through the night and possibly through many nights,' he said as he pulled into Maia's driveway.

Her house was at the end of a cul-de-sac and it was usually a quiet street. The neighbourhood was on the northern beaches, a reasonable distance from the city, and didn't attract big crowds, but tonight the front lawn was packed with cars and there were people everywhere. The place was teeming with uncles and aunts and cousins. Not a crowd, per se, just relations.

'It looks like Grand Central Station,' Todd said as he switched off the engine.

Maia frowned. It wasn't unusual to have dozens of people at their place; she had a large extended family and family gatherings were commonplace. Once a month they held a *hangi*, a traditional Maori barbecue, that all family members were invited to, but that was always on the last Sunday of the month which wasn't until the coming weekend. The only reason there could be so many people here today was because of the earthquake. She wondered what had happened. She hoped it wasn't the worst that she could imagine.

Todd had hopped out of the ambulance and had come around to open Maia's door for her. He waited for her to climb out and then kissed her goodbye. 'I can't come in. I have to get back to work.'

'That's okay, thanks for bringing me home.' She actually didn't mind that he couldn't come in. She wasn't sure she wanted him to. As selfish as it sounded, she didn't have the energy to spend on anyone else, even someone as undemanding as Todd.

She needed some time to herself, she needed some space. Looking at all the people milling around the house, she realised she probably wasn't going to get it, but she had to try to sort through her feelings.

Why hadn't Todd's kiss made her heart race? Why hadn't it left her wanting more? Why didn't he make her feel like Henry did? There was none of the same excitement or anticipation or feelings of new beginnings. And she knew it wasn't just because they'd been together for over two years. Todd had *never* made her feel that way. She had thought that perhaps it was just circumstances but, now that she had experienced it again with Henry, she knew that wasn't the case. Henry left her feeling breathless, alive, wanting more. It was almost impossible to drag herself away from him and her body responded immediately whenever he was near. She was aware of Henry on so many levels.

This was bad.

She hoped her feelings were just a culmination

of a stressful day. She was exhausted and emotionally fragile. She needed to sort herself out.

She gave Henry up three years ago. She couldn't have him back now. She needed to move on. She'd done it once. She could do it again.

By the following morning the power had been restored to Maia's house and to three quarters of the city but the restoration of power brought more bad news. Overnight the death toll had climbed to seventy-five, over two hundred people were still missing and the injury toll was in the thousands. Even more people had been made homeless either because their houses had been completely destroyed or because engineers had deemed the buildings unstable and therefore too dangerous to be in.

Her house had been total chaos. Not in the same vein as the devastation caused by the quake—her house hadn't been damaged in any way—but the chaos had ensued as a direct result of that because it was one of the few houses amongst her extended family that had escaped unscathed. Several relatives' houses hadn't been so lucky but fortunately no one had been badly injured. Accommodating an extra dozen or so was no problem and her cousins were happy to sleep on spare mattresses or camp in the garden.

But amongst the tales of woe were some remarkable tales of survival. After more than eighteen hours the Urban Search and Rescue teams were still finding survivors. People were being pulled from the wreckage alive. She knew that the first twenty-four to forty-eight hours were critical in that regard. After forty-eight hours, the chances of survival decreased rapidly until they were close to zero. Ninety-five per cent of people who survived entrapment were rescued within the first two days. The warm summer temperatures were a blessing, although that increased the effects of dehydration, but that could be counteracted as long as people were still alive.

Maia listened to the radio on her way into work. The bad news was interspersed with good but it was still difficult to listen to. There was so much pain and suffering, both physical and emotional, but she felt she needed to know what was going on. So much was happening so quickly. She almost thought she might prefer the bubble of denial that had been possible when there had been no power and limited communication.

The majority of the city still had no water and no sewerage, which meant infection control and gastroenteritis were going to be problems, along with the supply of fresh, safe drinking water. Even residents who had mains water were being advised to boil it twice before consuming it. Tourists were being evacuated, but at least the airport had reopened, which made that job a lot easier.

The community of Christchurch and the greater Canterbury area were rallying together as help came from further afield. Food and water were being brought in from other cities and the army had set up tents and temporary accommodation at several schools. Welfare centres had also been established at some of the local churches and sporting clubs, as well as the schools, and people were able to access food, water, shelter, and warm clothing and blankets. But just as importantly the welfare centres provided victims of the disaster with company and stopped the feeling of isolation that many displaced people experienced.

The aftershocks continued but they were lessening in frequency. There had been hundreds of small ones right through the night, but fortunately nothing like the main quake.

Maia waved to Brenda through her office window as she came into the ED. Brenda looked exhausted and Maia was surprised to find her still here. That could only mean that Keith hadn't been found yet, which wasn't good news.

The first order of the day would be a staff meeting to update the new shift about what was going on currently in the department. Maia headed for the kitchen. She'd make a coffee while she waited for the meeting to start. It would be her third of the morning. She was making up for the caffeine hits she'd missed yesterday due to the power outage. In lieu of a shower she'd made do with a swim in the pool at home and with a couple of coffees under her belt she suspected she might soon feel almost human.

She had just taken a mug from the cupboard when Henry walked into the kitchen. He had a surgical mask hanging from his neck and a theatre cap on his head. He snapped the ties as he walked into the room. He pulled the mask from his neck and threw it into the bin along with the cap.

Maia's heartbeat quickened at the sight of him. His dark hair was messy and he was unshaven. His beard grew quickly and the darkness of his stubble made his eyes look more blue and less indigo. She hadn't been able to forget the feel of his body under her fingers, the warmth of his skin, the firmness of his muscles or how it felt to be in his arms. She was having trouble sorting through her emotions. She knew it was partly because of the drama of the past twenty-four hours but the emotion was heightened by her reaction to him.

'You had an early start,' she said as she clicked a coffee pod into the machine and tried to ignore the traitorous stirrings of her body.

'I haven't left. I operated most of the night.' There was a plate of fresh sandwiches and another one of muffins on the table. Henry picked up a muffin. 'You got home all right?'

Maia nodded.

'And your family? Everyone is okay?'

'They're all fine. Some of them have lost their homes, so we've got a few extras camped out at our place, but everyone is physically okay.'

Maia handed him a coffee and his fingers brushed hers as he took it out of her hand. Maia had been expecting the contact, she'd prepared herself for it, but the shock of awareness still took her by surprise. She jumped and coffee slopped over the side of her mug.

Henry lifted a handful of paper serviettes from the dispenser in the middle of the table and passed them to her. She avoided his eyes as she cleaned up the mess, avoided looking at his lips as he bit into the muffin.

'Was Brenda here all night too?' she asked. 'She looked exhausted when I came in.'

Henry nodded.

'She must know that the Press Building collapsed?'

He nodded again.

'But there's been no news about Keith?'

'No.'

Maia sank into a chair as guilt swamped her. 'We should have said something yesterday. I should have told her about the Press Building. She might have been able to go into the city and find out more.' She'd said nothing to Brenda yesterday about the building. She'd been so busy but she also knew she'd chosen not to. She hadn't known anything definite and, as Henry had said, it wasn't her place to speculate. But she regretted it now. If she'd been in Brenda's shoes she would have wanted to know. 'I watched that building collapse,' she said. She was close to tears.

Henry stood up from the table and put his arms around her. She didn't resist his embrace. She rested her head against his chest and let him comfort her. It felt good. She didn't care if anyone walked in on them. Nothing was going to surprise people today.

'It's not your fault, Maia.'

'I know that but I should have said something. But if she knows now, why is she still at work? Why hasn't she been into the CBD?'

'She wasn't allowed in,' Henry replied. 'The CBD was closed off last night to everyone with the exception of emergency services.'

Maia had forgotten that, even though she'd seen it for herself when Todd had taken her home. But it didn't make it any easier. She wished now that she had said something. Guilt swamped her. Was it survivor guilt? Was she feeling guilty because she'd survived and so many hadn't? No, she refused to accept that Keith hadn't survived, not yet. But thinking of survivors made her think about Mark and Susan. She lifted her head to look up at Henry.

'What about Mark?' She was almost too scared to ask. Did she really want to know? What if it was bad news? 'Have you heard any news on him?'

Henry was nodding. 'I spoke to a mate at the Queen Liz this morning. He escaped without head or spinal injuries but they had to amputate his leg below the knee. But he made it through and by all accounts he's doing as well as can be expected.'

That was good news, in a way. She knew it was better than the alternative but it still wasn't great. Emotion and fatigue swamped her. She stepped out of Henry's embrace as the other ED staff members began to enter the kitchen ready for the morning update and wondered when the news would improve.

Brenda waited until the staff was assembled before telling them what they could expect this shift according to the S&R teams who were communicating from the exclusion zone in the CBD. Brenda looked wrecked but her voice was strong.

'Survivors are still being pulled from the rubble,' she said and Maia knew she was still hopeful that Keith would be amongst them. 'Like yesterday we expect to get the overflow from the general hospitals and the injuries will be at either end of the spectrum—minor injuries in those who might have been turned away yesterday and didn't present to the first-aid centres, or the more seriously injured if the other hospitals are at capacity and can't cope with the additional load. People are mainly presenting with fractures, respiratory conditions, concussion, dehydration and burns. I want you working in teams, as Henry outlined in his in-service, and there are job cards for everyone, including any ward staff we call in. As ED staff you will be the lead doctors and nurses for any cases.'

The meeting was short. Everyone knew their jobs. The routine was much the same as any other day with the exception being that many of their patients would be adults, not children. As Maia followed Henry and Brenda out of the meeting, she could hear them discussing the procedures for the day until Brenda paused midsentence and stopped in her tracks. Maia almost crashed into the back of her and, when she looked up to see what the problem was, she found two police officers waiting in their path. The officers—one male, one female—were holding their hats in their hands and they both had solemn expressions on their faces. They obviously were not here with good news.

'We're looking for Brenda Westin,' the female officer said.

Maia felt herself go pale as the blood rushed

out of her head, leaving her feeling light-headed. There could be only one reason they wanted to see Brenda.

Maia saw Brenda's knees buckle but fortunately Henry caught her before she hit the floor.

'This way,' Henry said to the police officers, leading the way to Brenda's office as he half carried her. Henry closed the door behind them and he and Maia sat on either side of Brenda, ready to support her. Introductions were made before the female officer continued.

'A number of bodies have been recovered from the Press Building,' she said.

Maia felt sick. She'd watched that building collapse.

'Keith?' Brenda asked. 'Have you found Keith?'

Brenda had gone pale and Maia thought she might either vomit or faint.

'We have a list of people who have been reported missing along with their last known location, but we haven't been able to positively identify all of the victims. That's why we are here. We want people identified—we need relatives to come to the morgue.'

Brenda started to shake. Maia wrapped an arm around her shoulders as she fought back tears.

'Are there any survivors still trapped inside?' Brenda asked, holding on to hope.

'The USAR teams are still searching. There are still people unaccounted for, so there could possibly be survivors, but nothing has been confirmed at the moment.'

Maia could hear in the police officer's voice that she thought it was unlikely that survivors would be found but she wasn't going to say as much.

'Do you have someone who can go with you? A family member?'

'My daughter is on her way here from Auckland. I have no idea what time to expect her. Transport is chaotic. I don't want to wait for her. I need to know if it's Keith.' She turned to Maia. 'I can't ask Louise to potentially ID her own father! I couldn't do that.'

'Of course not,' Maia agreed. 'Would you like me to come with you?' she offered. 'I know Keith.' She refused to use past tense.

'Would you?'

'Yes, of course.'

Carrie knocked lightly on the office door and as she entered Henry pulled Maia aside. 'Maia, it's not going to be anything like what you expect.'

'I know but I've seen plenty of dead bodies. I work in emergency.'

'I realise that, but these bodies will most likely be severely damaged. Some will be unrecognisable. The information I've received is saying that we will have to resort to DNA testing to identify some. It's not like seeing someone who has died of natural causes. It'll be worse than car accidents. Let me go with Brenda. I can't identify Keith but I can support Brenda. I know what to expect.'

Maia could see the pain in his eyes. Henry

had been in the same situation. He already had those memories.

Maia looked around the ED. It was still quiet. She knew Carrie would take Brenda's place as ED Director—she was the most qualified—so she asked, 'Carrie, if Henry and I take Brenda to the morgue, will you be able to manage without all three of us?'

'Sure. I can call in reinforcements from the wards as per Henry's disaster management plan.'

'Okay,' Maia said as she turned back to Henry. 'We'll all go.' She appreciated that he was trying to shield her but she doubted the process would be as easy for him as he was trying to make it out to be. He wanted to protect her but she also wanted to be there to support him.

'Where have you taken the victims?' she asked the police officers.

'We've had to move them to the morgue at the army base. Do you know where it is?'

Maia nodded.

'You'll need this pass.' The male police officer handed her a letter.

They took Brenda's car. Maia drove. She knew
where she was going. The Children's Hospital
was west of the city, the army base was to the
south. The streets weren't too badly damaged
on this side of the city but it was slow going due
to the detours. Traffic was being diverted to the
streets that could take the cars as whole other
sections of the city had been blocked off. They
drove in silence.

The letter gave them admission to the base
and the army chaplain met them in the administrative offices and accompanied them to the
morgue. Brenda declined his offer to accom-
pany her inside.

They introduced themselves to the army surgeon and the mortuary attendant, a routine
that felt civilised, yet slightly inappropriate. It
seemed ridiculous to observe the niceties of
society, given the circumstances, but maybe,
Maia thought, when your world was crumbling

around you those traditions became the glue that held you together.

The room was cold and brightly lit. It was like walking into a giant freezer. The walls were tiled and the concrete floor had a large drain in the centre. Maia didn't want to contemplate why the army had such a large and modern morgue.

A wall of drawers faced them and a row of stainless-steel tables lined the centre of the room. Two large sinks were positioned up against a glass window that looked into a smaller dissection room and surgical equipment—knives, saws and pliers—hung on the wall. The bright overhead lighting meant there were no dark corners, there was nowhere to hide. There was nowhere to escape the fact that death surrounded them.

Bodies had been grouped together depending on where they had been found. White sheets were draped over the corpses but most had their feet exposed. Tags had been attached to the toes of the victims noting where the body had been recovered from. There were five in a row with 'Press Building' written on the tag. The only further information was either male or female notation.

Maia took Brenda's hand in hers as the army surgeon led them to the first body in the group.

Brenda walked slowly along the line, looking at the feet. Maia walked with her, holding her hand. She could feel Henry behind them and she held her free hand out. She needed to have Henry with her too. He took her hand, reassuring her.

The fourth body in the line didn't have a toe tag. The feet were covered but the left hand was exposed and a tag was attached to a finger instead of a toe. It was a male hand. Maia could see neat fingernails, some age spots and a wedding ring.

Brenda stopped in her tracks. Her hand flew up to cover her mouth as she let go of Maia's hand. A choked sob escaped from Brenda's lips and Maia knew they'd found Keith.

Brenda stepped forward and picked up Keith's hand. The mortuary attendant was standing at the head of the table. He waited for Brenda to make eye contact with him before he folded back the sheet. Brenda closed her eyes as the attendant lifted the sheet and Maia heard her hold her breath.

From where she stood Maia could see the man's face. It was Keith. She felt Henry's silent query and nodded as tears welled in her eyes. The death toll had risen overnight to seventy-five, and with the bodies recovered today that toll was now even higher, but Keith was the first person that Maia knew personally to have lost his life. While she had friends and family members who were now homeless she hadn't, as yet, known anyone who had died.

Brenda's shoulders shook as she sobbed. She held Keith's hand and kissed his forehead. The mortuary attendant handed her a box of tissues as Maia hugged her.

'I'm so sorry, Brenda.'

The surgeon gave Brenda some time before he said, very quietly, 'Once you are ready, I'll need you to sign some paperwork.'

Brenda nodded but didn't look up, but eventually she was ready. Maia held her hand while she signed a form to formally identify Keith. 'Henry,' Brenda asked as she signed the papers, 'would you mind very much having a look at Keith? I need to know what his injuries are but I don't think I can bear to look myself.'

There was no report as yet so Henry had no choice but to look. He nodded and the mortuary attendant lifted the sheet once more. Maia saw Henry's expression change. He managed to keep his face neutral and it was only because Maia knew him well that she could see the tightening of his lips, the setting of his jaw, and she knew Keith's injuries were extensive. She wanted to go to Henry, to comfort him, but she couldn't leave Brenda.

Brenda had signed the papers and she gave

Keith another longing look. 'I don't want to leave him here alone,' she said.

'We'll wait outside and give you some more time with him,' Maia suggested. 'Take as much time as you need.'

There was a row of chairs lined up against the wall outside the morgue. Five chairs with plastic seats and metal legs had been welded together so that anyone sitting on one was within a few inches of anyone else. There was no personal space but fortunately Maia and Henry were the only ones there. Henry was very quiet.

'Was it very bad?' Maia asked.

Henry nodded. 'His legs and chest were completely crushed. He probably died from internal injuries. He would have lost a lot of blood and he would have been in a lot of pain. Hopefully he lost consciousness first.'

Henry leant forward propped his elbows on his knees and rested his head in his hands. He sighed, expelling the air from his lungs in a loud whoosh. He'd been up all night with barely a break and this situation had to be taking its toll on him also. Maia knew what would be on his mind. This wasn't the first time he'd been in a room filled with the bodies of victims of a natural disaster.

She put her hand on his thigh. 'Are you okay?'

'I'm fine.'

Somehow she doubted that. 'Do you want to talk about it?'

'What?'

'Your family. I know you must be thinking about them.'

He was thinking of them. Of course he was, how could he not be? The 2004 Boxing Day tsunami was never far from his thoughts and the events of today had ensured that those memories resurfaced. But he wasn't sure if he wanted to talk about it. Maia knew his history, she knew he'd lost his family in that tragic event, but he had never spoken about it in detail. Not to her or anyone else.

'Was it like that in Thailand?'

'God, no, it was much worse.'

But how did he begin to describe what he'd seen? It had been an enormous thing to get his head around when he'd arrived in Thailand a few days after the disaster. He had struggled even when seeing it first-hand. He still struggled with it. How would he explain it to someone who hadn't witnessed it? Why would he want Maia or anyone to have that picture in their head?

## CHAPTER NINE

HENRY HAD NEVER spoken to anyone about the horrors of the tsunami that had claimed the lives of his family.

It had happened six years ago but if he closed his eyes he could still picture it all so clearly: the devastation, the destruction and the dead. There had been hundreds of bodies laid out in rows in the corridors of the hospitals, in the street and in makeshift shelters. He could see it still and he could smell it. The stench had been the worst thing. The bodies of strangers he'd been able to cope with but the smell had been horrific and it was still so potent in his memory. He could smell it now and the foul stench made him want to retch.

He coughed and opened his eyes, bringing him back to the present to confront a new disaster.

'Are you okay?' Maia asked, concern etched in her deep, brown eyes. 'Do you want to go outside and get some fresh air?'

He took a couple of deep breaths. 'No. I'm all right.' He shook his head, trying to clear the images from his mind. He'd never spoken in detail of the devastation or of the horrors of having to identify his loved ones. He'd locked it away inside himself and used the power of that loss to spur him on to make a difference in disaster management. But he'd never dealt with the emotional trauma, he'd never been able to let it go, and it festered inside him and contaminated all his relationships. Being stoic and independent had cost him his relationship with Maia.

Had it been worth it?

He knew he'd made a mistake.

'What I saw in Thailand was far more traumatic than what we've seen here, but I'm not speaking on behalf of Brenda when I say that.

The next days or weeks or months aren't going to be easy for her or anyone else here—far from it—but the scale of the disaster will be more manageable, and the capacity of Christchurch and New Zealand to manage the catastrophe will be far better than in South-East Asia. Although, for the victims' families everything is relative, and for the people of Christchurch this is probably as bad as it gets. It'll certainly be the worst thing most of them have ever experienced and they'll need support to get through it.'

'And who was there to support you in Thailand?'

'Nobody,' he admitted. 'I thought I'd manage. I arrived in Thailand still pretending to be positive but it was already five days after the tsunami and I'd heard nothing. I hadn't completely given up. I hadn't wanted to believe the worst, but when I saw the devastation I knew it was hopeless. Roads were gone, trees were flattened, buildings destroyed, whole villages wiped out.

'Before I'd even had a chance to find my family, before I'd even got off the plane, I could see the damage and the chaos and I knew a miracle would be almost impossible. I'd refused to think of the worst-case scenario and that was a mistake. I'd seen photos in the news of the scenes but flying in and seeing the devastation was nothing like I'd imagined and I was completely unprepared. Pictures don't convey the smell, the chaos, the heartbreak, the despair.

'Huge boards had been erected displaying photos of the deceased and that was where we all started. There were hundreds of people searching for missing loved ones but so many of the deceased had drowned and were bloated beyond recognition, making identification difficult. My brother's picture wasn't on the boards, nor was my father's. I found my mother first and initially I'd been given false hope with reported sightings of my brother in one of the hospitals but it turned out to be another English boy. I had to go from hospital to hospital, morgue to morgue, school hall to school hall, searching and looking, and it took me two more days to find out anything at all. I kept hoping that entire time that my father and brother had survived but I eventually stumbled across my brother's body lying in a hospital corridor. That was the worst moment of my life. It was so unexpected and so confronting.'

'What about your dad?'

'His body has never been recovered. As awful as today was for Brenda, at least it was controlled. She had people she knew with her and she was semi-prepared to see Keith's body. She will have closure.'

'You shouldn't have come today,' Maia said as she tucked her arm through the crook of his elbow and reached for his hand. 'You should have let me look after Brenda.'

He squeezed her hand, grateful for the contact, grateful for the touch of a warm body. 'No, it's fine. Today hasn't upset me—it's brought back memories, certainly, but Thailand is never far from my mind and this was something I'd vowed to do after the tsunami. If I can help to ease other people's pain, either through treating victims and hopefully reducing the death toll, or at least supporting them when they need to identify loved ones, that is what I want to do. In Thailand, locals rallied and supported mourning Thais and tourists alike, and I know firsthand what a difference it can make just having another person there, even if they're a stranger, to lessen the loneliness and heartache, sadness and despair.'

Brenda emerged from the morgue as Henry finished speaking. She looked as though her heart was breaking. Maia's heart was breaking too, for Brenda and for Henry. She wanted to be able to fix them both but she knew there was nothing she could do. Brenda needed time and her daughter, and Henry wouldn't let her help him; he wouldn't let anyone close.

Despite the fact that years had passed for Henry he'd admitted the horrors of the tsunami were never far from his thoughts and Maia would bet every last dollar that he still hadn't dealt with the trauma. She knew it was that event that drove him in life. It was the tsunami and the loss of his family that had brought on his decision regarding his life plan and he was still on that path—the path to redemption. He was driven by guilt just as she was. Guilt that he hadn't been with his family, guilt that he hadn't perished with them, guilt that he'd survived. He didn't think he deserved to be happy and he didn't want to get close to anyone in case he lost them. He didn't think he could take that chance.

Maia and Henry took Brenda home and waited for her daughter to arrive before returning to work. Henry looked and sounded exhausted and spent most of the journey trying to stifle his yawns. Maia almost expected him to fall asleep in the car. It probably would have done him good. He'd worked all night and, while she thought he'd deny that the visit to the morgue had been harrowing, she suspected differently.

'I think you should go back to the hotel and

get some sleep,' she said as she turned into the hospital car park.

'I'm fine.'

She'd known he'd deny any problem but she wasn't prepared to give in. He really needed to take a break before he collapsed. Physically and emotionally. 'Henry, you're exhausted, you can't work like this.'

'If it's not busy when we get inside I'll have a kip in an on-call room.'

'Surely the hotel would be better?'

'I can't go back to the hotel. It's in the exclusion zone. It's still standing, but until the damage is assessed and its condition determined no one is allowed in. I can't even collect my things.'

Maia frowned. 'So where will you stay?'

'At the hospital. I'll camp out in an on-call room. I had a message from my rental agent this morning. I was supposed to be looking at accommodation on Saturday but that's been shelved. She says it will be difficult, if not impossible, to find somewhere to rent now. So many houses have been destroyed and thousands more so badly damaged that they will have to be demolished, which will make accommodation scarce.

'So many people are homeless and, although thousands have left Christchurch, there are thousands more who are staying but need somewhere to live. People can't live in the school gyms and in tents indefinitely. Other residents are all taking in extra people if they can. I'm not a priority. I'm one person who isn't injured and hasn't lost anything, really, except a suitcase and a few clothes.' He shrugged. 'I'll sleep here. Buy some clean underwear and a toothbrush from the hospital gift shop and wear scrubs.'

Maia felt terrible. She'd spent last night thinking about Henry but not in a practical sense. Her thoughts had all been ridiculous romantic fantasies. She hadn't spent one moment thinking about anything useful, like where he was sleeping.

She wanted to help. She knew he was lonely,

even if he wouldn't admit it. He professed to want to be alone but no one really wanted that, did they? She would help.

'Don't be silly,' she said. 'You can come and stay at our place. Half my extended family is camped out there. It's chaotic but if you can put up with that I'm sure I can find you a bed. We have no water, but there's a pool and the beach, and we do have power again. You can come home with me at the end of my shift.'

She didn't stop to think if she was making a big mistake. It wasn't until later that she wondered what had made her extend the invitation and what had made Henry accept. It had been a rash decision but they were the only sort she seemed to be able to make in her personal life. If she thought for too long about something, she ended up going around in circles, never coming to a decision. There were always too many things to consider and this situation was no different.

But she hadn't stopped to think. She'd just acted. And now she had to deal with the consequences.

Maia tied the straps of her black bikini top behind her back and adjusted the cups to make sure she was decent. She threw a red cotton caftan over her costume and headed for the beach. They still had no water and she needed a swim to wash off the sweat and the stress of the day. She could have taken a dip in the pool but the house was wall-to-wall people; it looked and sounded like a school camp site and the only way to get some peace and quiet after a distressing day was to head for the ocean. She opened the back gate and walked through the sand dunes onto the beach. The sand was warm under her bare feet and the air smelled of salt and seaweed. The ocean was dark blue against a paler sky and a gentle swell brought small waves onto the shore.

The beach was empty but for one other person.

She might not have complete peace and quiet but she didn't want it. Peace and quiet was only one attraction of the beach. The other one was standing in waist-deep water looking out to the horizon.

Henry.

He was all alone and once again she was struck by the thought that it wasn't right. No one should be completely alone. She'd seen the haunted look in his eyes after they'd been to the morgue. He'd said he was okay but there was no way on earth he could be. Not after today.

She stripped off her caftan and dropped it on the sand along with her towel.

The water washed over her toes. Despite the heat of the day the water was cool, and she stood in the shallows for a moment, acclimatising to the temperature as she watched Henry. He dived under a wave, not hesitating to get wet.

His head broke the surface of the water as he came back up. He turned around and pushed his wet hair back from his face. The beach faced east and at this time of the day the sun was low in the sky at Maia's back. The late-afternoon westerly sun hit Henry and the water glistened on his chest. He had removed the dressings that she had applied to his cuts yesterday and as he walked towards her she could see that the gashes on his chest and arm were already looking better. Her eyes travelled down the length of his body, following the trail of dark hair that disappeared under his board shorts. She had lent him a pair of her cousin's shorts as all his clothes were still quarantined in the hotel and the borrowed board shorts fitted him well. Extremely well. They sat snug on his hips and moulded to his thighs.

She shouldn't be looking.

She lifted her eyes back up to his face. His perfect face.

He was watching her too. She could see his eyes running over her curves and then his gaze came to rest on her breasts. She could feel her nipples harden. It was incredible. He didn't even need to touch her; just a look, just his indigo eyes caressing her, was enough to make her nipples peak and she could feel the warmth starting low in her belly and spreading outwards. She could feel every heart beat, every pulse, in her chest and throat and between her thighs. She was moist and shaky. Her reaction was enough to get her into the water. The cold ocean might calm her down before she did something stupid. Something she might regret.

Inviting him to stay had probably been a mistake but it was too late now. She'd have to deal with it. It was probably lucky that there were plenty of people around the house; there wasn't much chance that they'd be alone together.

Except for now.

Henry took another step towards her. She could see the desire in his eyes and knew it was reflected in her own. She needed protection from his gaze.

She dived under the water and started swimming, buying herself some time to think, hoping the cool water would settle her down. She stretched out parallel to the shore in a strong over-arm movement but she had no chance of leaving Henry behind. He was swimming beside her, matching her stroke for stroke.

After several minutes Maia stopped. She was breathing hard and needed to rest. She flipped onto her back and floated in the salty water. Henry was treading water next to her. She wanted to reach out and hold on to him. No one could see them, they were several hundred metres from the house, but she resisted the temptation. She wasn't in a position to do anything with Henry. She closed her eyes and tried to ignore the stirring of lust and desire in her belly.

She could feel him watching her. He hadn't said a word but he didn't need to. She had seen the desire mirrored in his eyes—she knew he was feeling it too.

She desperately wanted to reach out a hand to touch him but she knew that would open a door that she might not then be able to close. She knew that if she moved towards him he would meet her halfway, but she would be making him compromise his values as surely as she would be compromising her own. Once she stepped through that door, she would be turning her back on the promise she'd made to Todd, and to be disloyal to Todd was not something she wanted. She had to be strong.

Somehow she managed to resist him. She wasn't free to give herself to Henry no matter how much she wanted to. And that was the problem. She wasn't his but she still wished she was.

She had been pretending to herself that she was over him. It had been easy to fool herself when he was on the other side of the world, but having him back in Christchurch was proving to be torturous, and inviting him to stay was only going to make things worse. It might have been the most stupid thing she'd ever done. Possibly only trumped by letting him go the first time.

* * *

Maia was unsettled by the events of the past few days and weeks—the quake, Henry's return and her feelings for him, as well as her impending nuptials. Everything had changed and, while she knew none of this was really Henry's fault, he was certainly, as far as she was concerned, at the centre of it all.

She hadn't been able to rescind her invitation to him to stay with her family so she coped by trying to limit the time she spent with him, or at least making sure they had other company, whether at home or at work, but the awareness never left her. She tried hard not to be attracted to him but it was a difficult thing to deny.

She needed to be busy. And she was. She needed routine and order to make sense of the chaos in her head but there was no sense of order and routine at home. The quake had thrown everything into disarray. Part of her wished she could just float in the ocean for days, until everything was back to normal. But what was normal going to be?

It had been five days since the quake and there was still no running water or sewerage. Half of the buildings in the CBD were going to have to be demolished, if they hadn't already been destroyed, and the death toll stood at one hundred and twenty-three but more were still unaccounted for. There had been no survivors found for the past three days but people were still talking about miracles. One hundred and ten alone had been killed in collapsed office buildings, six had perished in buses that had been crushed and the rest had been killed by falling rocks and masonry. There were too many bodies and some still hadn't been identified. Because of the extent of the injuries, the experts were sometimes having to resort to using DNA from toothbrushes and hairbrushes, tattoos, dental records or fingerprints, as well as personal effects found on the bodies—wallets, keys and the like—in order to positively identify the victims.

It was going to take a long time for the city and her residents to recover. It was going to be a long time before things were back to normal and, for Maia, her sense of normal was about to change forever. She was getting married in three weeks.

Maia picked up another sweet potato as she tried to imagine walking down the aisle. At the moment it seemed almost impossible. Some things were continuing on as they always had but it was difficult to picture holding a wedding amongst the devastation, although they were managing to host the family's regular monthly Sunday night *hangi*.

Her mother had decided that since the majority of the family was already staying with them they might as well go ahead with the regular barbecue as there was food that had to be eaten. *'Hangi'* was the Maori word for 'earth oven' and the barbecue feast was traditionally cooked in a pit which Maia's dad had dug at the bottom of the garden where the grass met the sand dunes.

It was the men's job to get the fire started. It would take several hours for the wood fire to heat the volcanic rocks to a temperature high enough to create the steam that cooked the food, and while the oven was heating up the women prepared the food. Fish needed to be seasoned and wrapped in banana leaves, pork and lamb got wrapped in cabbage leaves, and potatoes and kumara were chopped up, placed in wire baskets, covered with wet cloth and then buried on top of the hot rocks and left to steam in the *hangi* for about four hours.

Maia was chopping sweet potato but she wasn't sure it was safe for her to be handling a sharp knife. She hadn't been eating or sleeping well since the quake; her concentration was shot and her hands were shaky. She was a bit of a mess. She was stressed over the wedding, her feelings for Henry and the changes to her world, both her immediate and larger worlds, brought by the earthquake and by Henry's return. Any one of those things was stressful enough to deal with and she was finding it difficult to cope with all of them en masse.

She had lost weight and was having recurring nightmares about the quake. The dream varied—sometimes she was trapped in the cathedral, sometimes she was on the street and would hear Henry calling her name, telling her to watch out as the cathedral tumbled around her, and sometimes she would be watching the walls fall around Henry. The dream varied but there were two things that were constant. She was always wearing her wedding dress—the irony hadn't escaped her that she hadn't actually chosen a wedding dress yet and she had no idea what to do about that, given that the dress shop had been flattened in the quake. The second constant was that it was Henry, not Todd, who was always in her dream.

She went to sleep each night worried that she would call out Henry's name and wake Todd. She lay awake for hours, feeling guilty that Todd was sleeping in her bed while she dreamt of

Henry. A guilty brain was apparently a restless one and she was finding sleep hard to come by.

The knife slipped off the edge of a kumara, narrowly missing her thumb. She handed the knife to Pippi before she caused herself an injury and started to layer slices of lemon on to the whole fish that had been stuffed and seasoned, before wrapping them in banana leaves. This was an easy job, one she didn't have to focus too hard on, which left her mind free to wander—and, of course, it went to Henry.

Not only was he in her dreams every night, she was spending far too many of her waking hours thinking about him too. He just had to look at her and her legs would turn to jelly, her heart would tremble, her pulse would begin to race, leaving her short of breath, and her temperature would rise. She could think of nothing else when he looked at her with his indigo eyes.

How on earth was she going to marry Todd when her heart desired Henry?

She needed to get out of the kitchen. She finished wrapping the fish and stepped out into the back garden. It was crowded with family and friends. It appeared that her sisters had invited everyone they knew, although Maia had also invited a number of extras. She looked around the garden. Todd was helping with the fire—it looked like they were almost ready to start cooking—and she could see Henry talking to some of her cousins, along with some of the hospital staff. Carrie was there along with Pippi's school friends and Lani's boyfriend, as well as a couple of ED staff. The air sang with the constant murmur of conversation and the frequent explosion of laughter.

For the first time since the earthquake people seemed relaxed. Except for Maia. Having Todd and Henry in the same place was keeping her on edge.

She longed to go and stand with Henry but she had vowed to keep a respectable distance. Her mother was sitting on the patio under the kiwi fruit vine. That looked like a safe spot to be.

She bypassed the ice boxes filled with beer—she wasn't drinking; she was worried that alcohol might loosen her tongue and she might say or do something she would regret—and sat beside her mum. 'What are you doing over here all by yourself?'

'Enjoying some solitude.' Neina laughed. 'In case you haven't noticed, it's been a mad house around here.'

Maia smiled. 'I had noticed.'

'I'm glad you're here,' her mum continued. 'I wanted to ask you about your wedding.'

'My wedding?'

'Yes. I assume since the damage caused by the earthquake you and Todd will have to adjust your plans and I just wondered what you've decided.'

'Nothing definite,' Maia replied. 'I'm thinking it might be easier to postpone it. It seems wrong to be planning a wedding when people are in mourning, but Todd is keen to make alternate plans. He thinks it will give us, and everyone else, something to look forward to, but there is so much that has to be reorganised. The cathedral has been condemned, so we can't get married there. The hotel where we booked our reception has structural damage and won't be repaired in time, although they've said they can move us into a marquee in their garden, and the dress shop where our dresses were coming from has been destroyed.'

Maia was still coming to terms with the fact that if Henry hadn't invited her to lunch then she might well have been in the dress shop that day. The shop had collapsed during one of the aftershocks so it was unlikely she would have been hurt but it was still a close call. 'And I haven't had a chance to find out about the florist yet. Basically, we have to start from scratch, and it's more than I can handle at the moment.'

Reorganising seemed like such a huge task. Maia wondered if all of these obstacles were signs indicating that they should delay the wedding or call it off, even. She had a reason to postpone it, but really it would give her a chance to work out what she ultimately wanted. 'I'm doing the right thing, aren't I? Getting married, I mean?'

'Only you can answer that.'

'You've always told us that you knew the moment you met Dad that he was the one. How did you know?'

'He made my heart sing,' Neina said simply. 'He brought me to life. I was only nineteen but I couldn't imagine my life without him and that never changed. He was the one I couldn't live without. I never looked at another man again and I can't imagine that I ever will. He was my life—him and you girls. He gave me everything I ever needed.'

'Do you think there's only one right person in the world for each of us?'

'No, I don't. But I do think that there's one person, above all others, who fits you best. It doesn't mean that you won't be happy with someone else. I think there is more than one right person, but perhaps only one *perfect* one for each of us. I was just lucky to find my perfect love first and I can't ask for anything more. No matter what we say, all of us are searching for love and happiness. If you can find that at least once in your life, you've done well.'

Maia was worried that her marriage might be the end of her chance at finding true happiness rather than the beginning. Her parents hadn't needed to look elsewhere, neither of them had needed anyone else, but Maia was afraid that one man wasn't enough for her. Unless that man was Henry. She was talking to her mother about Todd but she was thinking of Henry.

'You have to follow your heart,' her mother said just as Henry approached.

Maia had been acutely aware of his movements all day but had deliberately kept herself out of his vicinity. It was the only way she could cope with the chemistry that still burned between them. But he was heading straight towards them now and she knew there was no escaping.

He was dressed in a blue polo shirt that lightened his indigo eyes and a pair of casual shorts that showed off his long, powerful legs.

'Just the women I wanted to see,' he said as he took an envelope out of his shorts pocket. 'I have something for you.' He handed the envelope to Neina.

Maia's mother slid her finger under the flap and prised it open, pulling out a clutch of tickets. 'What are these for?'

'They are a thank-you for giving me a bed for the past few nights. The Canterbury Racing Association have organised a charity event to raise funds for the quake victims. It's a day at the races—lunch, champagne, fashion parades— so I booked a couple of tables in support and I'd like you to take one. I thought it might be a fun day out for you all.'

'That's a lovely idea, thank you, Henry.' Neina

stood and went to put the tickets somewhere safe, leaving Maia alone with Henry.

'Where did you get the tickets?' Maia asked him.

'Through Joanne Parker,' Henry replied. 'You remember her? She's an anaesthetist at the Queen Liz. She might have a room for me to rent. I was talking to her about that and she mentioned this fundraiser. Her brother is the CEO of Canterbury Racing.'

Maia did remember her. Joanne was petite, blonde, pretty and ran marathons. She was the polar opposite of Maia. She remembered Joanne very well and she wasn't happy to hear that Henry was considering moving in with her. 'I thought you didn't want to share accommodation.'

'I didn't, but accommodation is scarce at the moment, as you know. While I appreciate your hospitality, sleeping on your couch is hardly a long-term solution.'

'It's no problem,' she fibbed. The only problem was that Maia was having a hard time controlling her emotions. 'You're welcome to stay as long as you like.' But could the offer of a couch amongst a dozen other relatives compete with the offer of a bedroom at Joanne's place? Maia doubted it.

Henry smiled. 'That's very generous of you but I feel like I'm walking on eggshells.'

'What do you mean?

'I'm making you uncomfortable and Todd doesn't want me here.'

'It's not up to Todd.'

'If I'm going to be completely honest, I'm on edge too. I can't stand to see you with Todd but I know I can't compete. I have nothing to offer you.'

He could offer her his heart, Maia thought. And she would take it. But he had sworn years ago that he wouldn't give his heart to anyone.

Maia didn't want him to move out but she knew she was being selfish. Henry was being honest and she knew she couldn't say the same about herself. But if she was going to take a leaf out of Henry's book and be honest about how she was feeling what could she say?

Could she tell him that, even though he wouldn't let himself love her, she'd never really been able to let him go? Not completely. Could she tell him she'd been holding back a piece of her heart for him? That he had stayed in the back of her mind and in a corner of her heart for three years? That she had learnt to accept that he might always remain there, but that she was still hoping that one day she would meet the man who would fill her whole heart? That one day she might meet the man who would be able to wipe all traces of Henry from her heart and mind, but that Todd wasn't that man? That she'd been so afraid of being alone that she'd accepted Todd's proposal, but she knew now that logic and reason couldn't replace passion and love?

But she said none of those things. She wasn't in a position to tell him how she felt.

* * *

The racecourse looked gorgeous. It was a glorious early-autumn day. The sun shone in a cloudless blue sky, the freshly cut grass was a bright emerald green and the roses bloomed along the racetrack railing. The Canterbury racecourse was only eight kilometres from the city but there was no sign of the devastation wreaked by the quake out here. It was almost possible to forget what had happened just a little under two weeks ago.

Carrie had insisted that they use Henry's gift and she had planned a girls' day out which included Maia's mum and sisters and a few other girlfriends. In the end Maia had embraced the idea. She needed something to look forward to. She needed to let her hair down and have some fun and that was what she intended to do. She would forget about the wedding and the quake and all the things she'd been refusing to deal with. Everything could wait for another day.

She'd taken care with her outfit. She had chosen a stiff cotton sateen dress with a fitted sleeveless bodice and a flared skirt. It was white with large roses in varying shades of pink printed on it. Ariana had fixed her hair into a French bun and tucked frangipani flowers into her dark tresses. She'd completed the look with white strappy sandals, a pink clutch, bright pink lipstick, and a dash of mascara and blush. It was nice to make an effort, especially when she felt like she hadn't worn anything except her uniform, scrubs or bathers for two weeks, but who was she making an effort for?

Henry was seated at the table beside hers. He had filled the second table with his friends and Maia was trying to ignore him. She was trying to pretend he was just a handsome stranger at the adjacent table but that was almost impossible. His table was so close to hers that if he leant back in his chair his shoulder could brush against hers. Maia was totally aware of every movement he made, every conversation he had, every time someone laughed at one of his remarks. She tried to pretend his proximity wasn't affecting her but she'd been unable to focus on anything but his scent—citrus and cedar—the sound of his voice—quiet, deep and tuned just for her ear—and the way the air stirred around her every time he moved. How could she concentrate on anything else when he was near? There was no way of ignoring him or her reaction to him.

And, along with trying to pretend she was immune to Henry, she was also trying to pretend that Joanne wasn't sitting next to him—young, pretty, intelligent and recently divorced Joanne, whom Henry had moved in with just a few days ago. Maia refused to admit she was jealous. She knew she had no right to be. Nor would she admit that she missed having him around. But that hadn't stopped her from carefully considering her outfit.

She'd been surprisingly nervous about spending the day with Henry, while trying to maintain a respectable distance, but her nerves had diminished with her first glass of champagne.

Or maybe it had been her second. She couldn't remember how many she'd had.

As the waiter cleared her plate Maia studied the form guide, pretending to be immersed in the finer details of horse racing when she actually had no idea what any of it meant.

'Are you going to place a bet?' Henry was standing behind her, leaning over the back of her chair, and the sound of his soft, deep voice in her ear sent a tingle along her spine.

She squeezed her knees together as the deep timbre of his voice lit a fire between her thighs. 'I was thinking about it,' she said as she looked up at him. 'But I might as well just give my money to the bookie. I have no idea what I'm doing.'

'Would you like to go and take a look at the horses? One might catch your eye that way.'

'You can see the horses?'

'Of course.' He smiled, making the dimple in his chin disappear. 'You can walk past the stables, and before a race the horses are paraded around the mounting yard.' He checked his watch. 'There should be some coming out about now for race four.'

Maia knew it wouldn't help her with her betting but if it meant a chance to have Henry to herself, away from the watchful eyes of her family and away from Joanne, she wasn't about to refuse that invitation. She was sure Joanne was perfectly nice but not for Henry.

She pushed her chair back, picked up her handbag and prayed that her shaky legs would support her, but as Henry led her across the third-floor function room towards the lift she hesitated. 'Can we take the stairs instead?' she asked. She knew the emergency exit stairs were on the opposite side of the room. She'd come up that way. Since the earthquake she'd avoided elevators. She had a fear of getting trapped in a lift during an earthquake, and as the city was still experiencing aftershocks another quake was highly likely. Her sandals had high heels, but it was only three flights of stairs, and walking in high heels was preferable to being cooped up in a lift. Just in case.

He held the door for her and as she brushed past him she could feel the warmth of his breath on her neck. She gripped the railing as she willed her legs to keep moving. She focused on the stairs. One foot in front of the other. One step at a time. She knew how to get down a flight of steps.

They were halfway down when she stumbled.

Henry put his arm around her waist to steady her. 'No more champagne for you,' he teased.

His touch sent the now familiar surge of longing through her. She knew he was holding on to her to support her but his touch only made her more unsteady on her narrow heels as her hormones surged and her heart raced. She gripped the stair railing more tightly in an attempt to counteract the wobbliness that Henry's touch had triggered and felt the railing vibrate as she took another step. The vibration travelled through her, compounding her instability, then she heard the familiar, accompanying sound. She paused, frozen on the step, one foot in mid-air as the earth grumbled and groaned.

'Did you hear that?' she asked.

She let go of the railing and turned towards Henry, thinking she'd rather be hanging on to him, when the staircase moved underneath her and the lights flickered and went out. Her arms shot out, reaching for something to hold on to. It was an instinctive reaction, elicited by the darkness and the odd sensation of a moving staircase. But she was grabbing at nothing.

The staircase disappeared from beneath her feet and she pitched forward into the shadows.

She was falling.

She was tumbling.

She was plummeting headfirst into the darkness.

Somewhere over and above the noise of falling concrete and rumbling earth she heard the sound of her own voice. She was calling for Henry.

Her arms were flailing but her hands and arms were making contact with nothing.

There was no railing and no Henry.

There was nothing there.

Nothing at all.

# CHAPTER TEN

MAIA CRASHED WITH a thump onto the concrete landing between the two flights of stairs, expelling the air in her lungs in a loud 'whoosh' as she hit the ground. Somehow she managed not to hit her head but her left leg twisted underneath her; she came down hard on top of it and heard something crack. Searing pain shot up her leg and she thought she might pass out.

'Maia?'

Hearing Henry's voice calling her name was enough to keep her in the present but she was unable to speak. She was completely winded and gasping for air.

She couldn't breathe. She couldn't talk and she couldn't see either. The stairwell had no windows and now no lights. They were in complete darkness.

'Maia?' She heard Henry's voice again and felt his hand on her arm.

'Maia?'

She could hear a note of panic in his voice now. He was probably wondering if she was dead or alive. She still hadn't been able to catch her breath, she still couldn't speak, but she thought she might be able to move her arm. She bent her elbow, sliding her arm up until her hand was under his palm and then curled her fingers around his.

'Oh, thank God.'

The emergency lights above the exit doors came on as she heard Henry's sigh of relief. An eerie half light lit the dusty stairwell, barely illuminating their surroundings. The lights had a green tinge which made them look a little weird, like motion-sick aliens.

Henry's hand was on her chin; his fingers cupped her face and stroked her cheek. 'Maia, sweetheart, are you okay?'

She shook her head as the dust settled and she

finally managed to gasp a lungful of air. Something hurt but it was hard to focus while Henry's fingers held her face.

Something was throbbing. She closed her eyes and concentrated on the pain. Her ankle. She opened her eyes and glanced down her leg, pointing towards her foot. She could see that her ankle was already starting to swell, and she thought she could see some purplish bruising, although it was difficult to be certain due to the ghostly green lighting. She sat up, trying to get into a more comfortable and less awkward position, but gasped in pain as she moved her left leg.

'Careful.' Henry dropped his hand from her face and took her by the shoulders, supporting her as she tried to sit up. He pulled his phone from his pocket and swiped the screen. A bright light beamed from the end of his phone as he activated the flashlight app. He scanned her with the light. 'God, Maia, you're bleeding.'

Maia looked down at her dress, the front of

which was covered in blood. She had no idea how that had got there. She took a deep breath and her lungs filled with air. She could breathe easily now. There was no pain in her chest. At least there was nothing wrong there.

She lifted her hands and turned them over as Henry shone the light on her palms. Her palms were wet with blood, sticky but not sore. The blood was running down from her elbows. She'd taken the skin off the back of both her forearms when she'd crashed to the ground, but that pain was minimal in comparison to her ankle.

Henry took a handkerchief from the pocket in his jacket and wiped the blood away.

'That's not too bad.'

'Not as bad as my ankle,' she told him. It was funny how blood always caught the attention, yet she knew those injuries were minor.

The light from Henry's phone illuminated her left ankle which, in the past minute, had ballooned to twice its normal size.

Henry passed her his mobile. 'Can you hold this for me while I have a look?'

She took the phone and kept the light trained on her leg as Henry slid his hands gently down from her knee to the lower third of her shin. He ran his fingers along her tibia to the inside of her ankle. His fingers were soft, his hands gentle and his touch made the pain bearable. It receded into the background as she imagined how it would feel to have Henry's hand roam over the rest of her body.

'How's that?'

*Fantastic*, she almost said. 'That's all fine,' she said. 'But I felt something crack when I landed.'

Henry sat on the bottom step—it was about all that remained of the staircase—and lifted her foot into his lap. The heel of her shoe hung limply from the sole. It must have snapped when she rolled her ankle. He carefully slid her sandal from her foot and palpated gently below her lateral malleolus and over the bones of her foot. None of that bothered her but when his fingers moved up over the bump of her ankle she thought she might pass out with the pain.

'There,' she gasped.

'I think you might have a fractured fibula. Not compound, thankfully. You'll need an X-ray but hopefully it's nothing worse than that. Nothing else is hurting?'

'No,' she said as she shook her head. 'But I don't think I can stand on it.' The thought of putting any weight on that leg made her feel nauseous.

'That's okay, I'll carry you, but I have to see which is the best way out of here first.'

Henry took care putting Maia's foot on the ground before he stood up. Using his flashlight app, he could see down the stairwell. A pile of concrete, the remains of the stairs, lay on the next landing, completely blocking the remainder of the staircase and the door. The door opened into the stairwell; there would be no easy exit that way.

He shone the flashlight up but there was nothing above them. The stairs they had been standing on had totally disappeared but for the very last one. There must have been a weakness in the concrete—he could see the smooth edge where two sections had been joined and one section was now lying a whole flight below where it should be. The lower exit was blocked, so there was no point going down, but he couldn't go up either.

Looking at the mess, he knew it was lucky they hadn't been crushed. He hated to think what could have happened to them if they'd been standing on the other half of the staircase. They were lucky to have escaped serious injury. A broken ankle seemed manageable when confronted with the reality of being trapped in a concrete tomb.

He checked the screen of his phone. There was no reception. They were stuck here until someone found them.

'Can we get out?' Maia asked.

He shook his head. 'No. The door is blocked

on the floor below us and there's nothing above us.' For all intents and purposes they were imprisoned in a concrete bunker. Not a tomb—he knew they would be rescued eventually; it was only a matter of time—but, for now, they were stuck.

'Can you call someone?'

He shook his head again. 'No reception,' he said as he held his phone up.

'How are we going to get out? If you've got no reception, how will they know where to look?'

'They'll know we're missing, the others will tell them. They'll keep searching until everyone is found.'

'That's assuming everyone else is okay.'

'Come on, Pollyanna, we'll be fine.' He tried to make light of the situation but the reality was he had no way of knowing what the situation was outside the stairwell. 'Someone will find us.'

'What's on these floors?' she asked.

'I have no idea. Offices, I think. Maybe store-rooms.'

'So no one will hear us if we yell?'

'Maybe not yet, but someone will come even-tually, and in the meantime I will take care of you.' He could hear the trace of panic in Maia's voice. He didn't want her to panic. It was his job to protect her. She had to know he wouldn't let anything happen to her.

But, his conscience argued, he already had, hadn't he? She was lying in front of him with a broken ankle.

He was still standing on the step. He shrugged out of his jacket and hung it over the section of bent and twisted stair railing that hadn't fallen into the abyss. He stripped off his shirt.

'What are you doing?'

'I'm going to bind your foot for you. It might make it more comfortable. And then you should keep it elevated.'

He bit the button off one of his cuffs. He didn't want to press the button into her swollen leg.

He squatted down and picked up her foot. In the light of his phone he could see that her toenails were pale pink; they looked like tiny shells glued to the end of her brown toes. Her skin was soft and warm. He cupped her foot in his hand and wound the sleeve of his shirt around her foot and up her leg, followed by the body of the shirt, compressing her lower leg, and finally he wrapped the other sleeve over the top and tucked the end in.

'Better?' he asked as he rolled his jacket up.

'Yes, much better, thank you.'

He put his jacket on the bottom stair and propped Maia's foot on top of the temporary cushion, elevating it.

He switched off the flashlight app to conserve his battery and sat with his spine against the wall, pulling Maia back so she could lean on him. It was stuffy and airless in the stairwell but at least he didn't have to worry about them being cold.

The air smelled of frangipanis. Maia had

tucked the flowers into her hair. He breathed deeply; the scent was familiar and pleasant. He was more than happy to sit there for as long as it took with Maia lying against his chest.

'Do you think we should try making some noise? Someone might hear us.'

'I'm in no hurry to get rescued,' he said as he tightened his arms around her ever so slightly. 'I've got everything I want right here.'

Maia didn't reply, she just looked up at him with her enormous brown eyes. In the dim half light of the emergency lighting, he saw her throat move as she swallowed. When she kept her eyes focused on him and licked her lips, he almost groaned aloud with desire. He wanted her more than he had wanted anything else in his life.

He had panicked when Maia had plummeted down the stairs and he'd felt his heart stop momentarily with fright before the adrenalin had made it beat so hard in his chest, he'd thought it was about to burst through his skin.

It had stopped again when he'd found her lying on the stairs. He'd lost everyone he'd ever loved and he couldn't lose her too. He realised then that he couldn't let her go. Not now. He'd been given a second chance and only a fool would let her go twice. He was no fool—a bit misguided, perhaps, but not a fool—and he had a chance now to put things right. He couldn't bear to lose her, either to Todd or through his own doing. He had to claim her. If he didn't claim her he would lose her altogether.

He shifted a little to move around to her side. Her hair had come loose from the bun at the nape of her neck. As he brushed it back from her face, a flower came loose and fell into his hand. He lifted it to his face and inhaled its scent, knowing frangipanis would forever make him think of Maia.

He put it on the ground beside him and ran his fingers along the side of her face. He heard her sharp intake of breath as his thumb traced over her lips.

Her lips moved under his thumb. 'What are you doing?'

He bent his head towards her. 'What I've wanted to do since the night I got home.'

'We shouldn't,' she breathed but her voice was just a puff of air. It lacked any conviction.

'I don't think we can stop it.' His voice was a whisper in the silence of the stairwell. His heart had only just resumed its normal rhythm and now, under Maia's gaze, he could feel it starting to increase in tempo again. He could feel the blood pounding in his veins, flooding all his extremities, throbbing in his groin.

She was intoxicating and he was filled with longing, light-headed with need, burning with desire. 'I want you, Maia, more than I've wanted anyone or anything in my life, and I think you want me too. There is still chemistry between us. Plenty of it. I know you feel it. I can hear it in your voice and I see it in your eyes. I've felt it in the air and in your touch. This is our opportunity for a second chance.'

Another frangipani flower fluttered to the floor as Maia shook her head. 'It's too late. *You're* too late.'

'No, I'm not. Don't marry Todd,' he begged. 'Not if you still love me.'

'You were everything to me, Henry, but you chose a different life. You chose to save the world. You didn't choose me.'

'That was my mistake,' he said as he picked up the fallen flower and tucked it behind her ear. 'And I won't make the same mistake twice. Don't write me off. You know what the tsunami did to me—you know why I made the choices I did, why I needed to feel like I was making a difference. But these quakes have shown me that my life means nothing, my plans and goals and promises mean nothing, if I don't have you. Before I met you I was prepared to be alone. I thought I could manage—I thought I could deal with the loneliness, I thought that was what I wanted. I didn't want to love another person. In my mind loving people left me open to heartache and loss, and I didn't want to risk losing anyone else I cared about but I can't live without you. I don't want to. I would rather tempt fate than give you up voluntarily.'

'Oh, Henry, you have no idea how I missed you. How I longed for you. How I wished it was your arms around me. How I wished it was you in my bed at night, but it wasn't, and eventually I had to stop wishing. I had to move on with my life and Todd was there for me when I needed him.'

*And you weren't.* Henry heard her unspoken words but he wasn't done yet. 'Maia, don't do this. Give me another chance. Give us another chance. I couldn't give myself to you back then, I had nothing to give. I needed to save the world, to fight my demons, but I should never have left you. It was foolish of me to think that you might still be here, that you might still want me.'

'I did want you, Henry, more than I ever wanted anything.'

'And now? Do you still want me?' His heart

felt as if it had lodged in his throat while he waited for her answer. He couldn't believe how nervous he was.

'I'm committed to Todd,' she said as his heart sank into his stomach and nausea replaced nervousness. 'I made my father a promise and I have given Todd my word. I know it was my father's wish for me to marry Todd. When he asked Dad's permission to marry me that was one of the last moments that Dad was truly happy before he died. How could I refuse Todd's proposal after that? How could I do anything else?'

'You're settling for a life that you think your dad wanted for you, but surely he would want you to be happy? Is this marriage going to give you the life you wanted? Is it going to make you happy? I'm begging you, Maia, please, don't do it. Don't marry Todd.'

'And what about when this disaster is over?' she asked. 'You'll want to move on to the next disaster and then the next. What will happen to me then? To us?'

'You can come too. Or I'll stay here. I'll do whatever you want if you'll agree to spend the rest of your life with me. I came back for you and I don't want to lose you. Not to an earth-quake and not to another man. You've taught me to love again and now I'm more afraid of losing you than of risking my heart. If I were to lose you I would have lost everything.'

'I've made a promise to Todd.'

Could he hear her resolve weakening or was that just wishful thinking?

'There's no law that says you can't change your mind. It's all up to you. You can't tell me that you and Todd share the same chemistry that we have. You can't tell me there's nothing between us. We both feel it. Do you think Todd wants to be your second choice? You can choose your happiness or choose to spare Todd's feel-ings. You can choose our happiness or choose to keep a promise you think you made to your father,' he said as he ran his hand over the edge of her jaw and let his fingers trail down her neck until his hand was on the bare flesh of her arm.

He heard her sigh and knew he wasn't playing fair but he was a desperate man. He had one last chance. 'It's your choice, but I don't want to live my life without you. I need you. I love you.' His thumb traced the outline of her mouth. 'Marry me instead, Maia.'

Her face was still tilted up towards him. She was shadows and light. She had a bruise on her cheek and there was a question in her dark eyes, but a smile on her pink lips. He bent his head. There would be time for talking later.

His lips covered hers. She closed her eyes and sighed and, as the sigh escaped, her lips parted and he took that as an invitation. He deepened the kiss. His tongue explored and delved and tasted. She tasted of champagne and strawberries, of bubbles and goodness. She smelled like frangipanis, of summer and sweetness. She was soft in his arms. She felt like home.

* * *

Maia slid a hand behind Henry's head as he deepened the kiss, holding him to her as her body responded and the memories flooded back, and she remembered how life had felt when she'd been with Henry. Nothing had ever come close, before or since. She thought she'd been coping but now she realised she'd only been surviving, only half-living. A piece of her heart had wilted when Henry had left but now that little piece of her blossomed again, like wildflowers after rain. She could feel herself unfurling as blood pumped through her heart, flooding that wilted piece, and her body came to life. She could feel the power of his kiss repairing her heart and making it beat properly for the first time in years.

She had one hand behind his head and the other on his arm. His muscles were warm and solid under her fingers.

He tasted of peppermint. He smelled like grapefruit and cedar. He felt like her future.

She loved him still. She'd never stopped. She would wait for her heart to heal and then she would give it back to him.

*'Hello?'*

He felt Maia jump in his arms as a voice called down from above them. She pulled away, leaving Henry wanting more, but their time was up. The door to the flight above them had opened, the door to the flight of stairs that was no longer there, and the voice called out again.

'Hello? Is there anyone in there?'

'Down here,' Henry replied.

He was reluctant to leave Maia but he had no choice. He took a long look at her face. Her dark eyes were huge and solemn, her lips pink and swollen from being thoroughly kissed. She looked utterly gorgeous but sad. As he stood up he sensed that this was the end. They both knew it. Once he got up he might never get another chance to hold her in his arms but he couldn't prolong their isolation. Maia needed medical attention.

Henry directed the rescue mission. Because of Maia's ankle, they couldn't winch her up the stairwell—the angles didn't allow access with a stretcher—so the only way out was through the blocked lower-level door. Two firemen were lowered into the stairwell and together the three of them cleared the rubble. If anyone wondered why Henry hadn't started until now, no one voiced the question, but finally they had cleared enough space to allow them to open the door.

Todd was on the other side. Waiting. A reminder to Henry that Maia wasn't his.

Henry climbed the steps and returned to Maia. He picked up the fallen frangipani flower and put it in his pocket before scooping her up and carrying her down the stairs. He buried his face in her hair and took a last, deep breath, inhaling her scent as he paused, before getting ready to step over the last blocks of concrete. 'Choose me, Maia. Be mine,' he whispered to her as he carried her out of the stairwell.

It was time to hand her over but he couldn't

bring himself to hand her to Todd. He laid her gently on the stretcher instead but even that felt like he was giving her up.

He followed the stretcher outside and watched as she was loaded into the ambulance. He waited for her to call to him, to ask him to go with her, but she said nothing. Her dark eyes kept him in sight until the doors were closed but there were no last words, no last-minute declarations. He took the frangipani flower from his pocket and held it to his nose as the ambulance drove away. He didn't want to believe this was the end but there was nothing more he could do. If Maia chose to marry Todd, Henry knew he would have to leave Christchurch. He couldn't stand the thought of seeing her but not being able to have her. He wasn't prepared to live his life watching Maia with another man.

The ambulance doors slammed into place, forming a solid, impenetrable barrier, separating Maia physically from Henry and taking her by surprise. Was he letting her go? Again? Were all his words just empty promises, platitudes? Was he going to let her leave?

Her fragile heart sat heavily in her chest. She wasn't sure if she was strong enough to cope with this. But what had she expected? Had she expected Henry to make a scene? To sweep her off her feet? To chase after her and swear his devotion while Todd sat in the ambulance beside her? Did she expect him to ignore Todd's part in this tableau? She knew he wouldn't do that.

Henry had been watching her closely as she'd been loaded into the ambulance. His blue eyes had been dark, unsmiling, haunted. He'd been watching her and waiting. She'd assumed he had more to say but now she realised he had said everything he needed to. He'd told her how he felt. He'd been honest. She could scarcely believe he'd come back for her. After all those years of waiting, of wondering how he really felt, he'd actually come back for her.

He loved her.

With every metre of distance the ambulance put between her and Henry, Maia could feel her heart tearing and breaking piece by piece. The freshly healed fragments of her heart weren't yet strong enough to cope with the pull of separation. As the ambulance carried her further away she realised he'd been waiting for her to speak. It was her turn now. The next move was up to her.

She wanted to tell the ambulance to stop, to turn around, to take her back to Henry. She could feel her future slipping out of her grasp with every yard, every corner, every street. Henry *was* her future. She couldn't give him up again.

What happened next was definitely up to her. She had to take the chance. She had to know she had done everything she could. She had to know how this ended.

She put her hand on her chest as if she could physically hold her heart together and two fat tears spilled from her eyes and rolled down her cheeks.

'Do you want something for the pain?' Todd's voice was earnest, his eyes kind and concerned.

She shook her head. It wasn't her ankle that was troubling her.

She looked at Todd and knew Henry was right. She was settling for a life that other people had wanted for her. She loved Todd but she wasn't in love with him. She'd been trying to fill a void left by her father's death and by Henry. She hadn't wanted to be alone, and Todd had solved that problem, but it wasn't the answer she was looking for. Life with Todd would be fine, she'd be okay, but she wanted more than fine—she wanted more than okay. She wanted it all. She wanted passion, laughter, love and joy. She wanted Henry.

'Is there anything you need?' Todd asked.

She nodded.

She needed Henry.

She didn't want to hurt Todd but her heart

belonged to Henry. It always had and Todd deserved better than to be her second choice. He deserved to have someone who loved him unconditionally and completely. Todd was a good friend, a good man, but Henry was the one she couldn't live without. She had to fix this before she ruined everything.

She slid her engagement ring off her finger and pressed it into Todd's palm. 'There's something I need to tell you…'

# EPILOGUE

MAIA FLEXED HER ankle as she sat in front of the mirror at her mother's dressing table. It was six weeks since she'd fractured it and she'd finally been allowed to take the moon boot off yesterday. Her ankle was stiff, she'd be walking with a limp, but at least she was walking.

An envelope with her name on it lay on the dressing table. She recognised Todd's handwriting on the front. She opened the envelope and read the short note, finishing just as her mother came into the room. She slipped the letter back inside the envelope and stuck it in the mirror.

'Is everything all right?' Neina asked.

Maia lifted her head and met her mother's gaze in the mirror. 'Everything's perfect,' she said. 'Todd was just sending his best wishes to us both.'

Neina slid Maia's wedding dress off its hanger and said, 'He's really okay with your decision?'

'He said he wasn't going to stand in the way. He could see that what Henry and I have is special. He wants that too. He deserved better than to be my second choice, my consolation prize.'

Maia held her arms up in the air as her mother slipped the simple, white satin sheath over her head. The fabric slid easily down her body, skimming her hips and falling to her ankles.

'Ready?'

Maia nodded as she removed the silk scarf that protected her hair and make-up and picked up her wedding bouquet, a simple spray of white orchids from her father's greenhouse interwoven with clusters of frangipani flowers, and walked with her mother along the path that led from their house to the beach.

White chairs had been set up on the sand and a space had been left through the middle, marking out an aisle. The aisle was lined with hurricane lamps, and fairy lights had been strung between poles that formed a border around the rows of seats. At the end of the aisle a simple wooden platform covered with a white muslin draped roof had been erected.

Maia could see Carrie and her sisters. Everyone was waiting for her. Her mother kissed her on the cheek. 'Be happy, my darling,' she said.

Maia hugged her mother tightly. 'Thanks, Mum,' she said, before waiting as Neina went to join her other daughters.

Maia would be walking down the aisle alone. But that was how she'd wanted it. A simple wedding, at home, with her family and friends. She didn't need anyone to walk her down the aisle. Everything she needed was waiting for her at the end of the sandy path.

She lifted her eyes and smiled at her fiancé.

Henry beamed back at her. He wore linen trousers and a simple white shirt. His skin was tanned and his indigo eyes were dark. Like her he was barefoot. She was having the simple wedding she had dreamed of; today was a celebration of their love and the beginning of their life together.

In the end her decision had been easy. In the end she hadn't really had a choice. She couldn't imagine living her life without Henry. She knew to have decided anything else would only have ended up hurting the people she cared about, Todd and Henry, both in different ways.

She moved down the aisle, past Brenda and her hospital colleagues; past Carrie; past her uncles, aunts and cousins; her mum and her sisters. She wasn't having attendants; she didn't need anyone other than Henry.

He was waiting for her under the muslin-draped roof. The late-afternoon sun shone on him, lighting the way forward. The air around her shifted and stirred as she got closer to him. It carried the scent of cedar and citrus to her and brought a feeling of anticipation and excitement. It whispered to her. It brought her home.

Henry reached for her as she stepped up onto the platform. A tingle ran along her spine and her nipples tightened in a visceral reaction to his touch. Her body had its own way of telling her what she wanted. But her head and her heart and her body all agreed. She wanted Henry.

The priest cleared his throat and Maia tried to focus as Father Alex began the service. She barely remembered walking down the aisle—all she could think about was Henry—but she did remember her vows. She hadn't had to rehearse them; she spoke from her heart.

'My heart belongs to you, Henry Alexander Cavanaugh. You are the man I can't live without. I promise to love you, respect you and be honest with you all the days of my life.' She waited for Father Alex to hand her the ring. 'In the name of the Father, the Son and the Holy Spirit,' she said as she slid it onto Henry's finger.

Then it was Henry's turn. 'Maia Grace Tahana, thank you for agreeing to be my wife. I promise to love you and to share the rest of my life with you, to always be there for you and to be the best person I can be. For you.' He took the ring from Father Alex and touched it to the ends of her fingers as he continued. 'I promise to love you, cherish you and take care of you for the rest of our lives.'

Then Father Alex said the words Maia had been waiting to hear. 'I now pronounce you husband and wife. You may kiss your bride.'

Henry cupped his fingers under her chin and lifted her face up to his. Maia wrapped one hand around Henry's head and pulled his lips down to hers as she gave him her heart and soul.

As Henry kissed her Maia knew he would never let her go again. She could taste all his promises for their future together in that one kiss.

He smiled at her as their lips parted. 'I love you, Mrs Cavanaugh,' he whispered.

'I love you too, my husband.'

* * * * *